Little Lit

IT WAS A DARK AND SILLY NIGHT...

OUR WRITERS AND ARTISTS ALL STARTED THEIR STORIE

IT WAS A DARK A

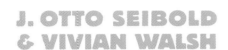

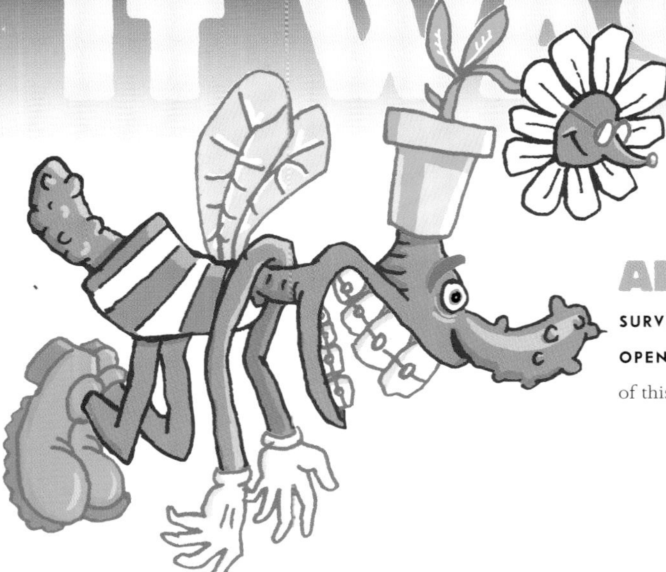

COVER

ART SPIEGELMAN is the Pulitzer Prize-winning author of **MAUS: A SURVIVOR'S TALE,** an account of his parents' experiences in the Holocaust, as well as a children's book, **OPEN ME...I'M A DOG!** Art lives in Manhattan with his wife, **FRANÇOISE MOULY,** the co-editor of this book and the art editor of **THE NEW YORKER**. They have two children, Nadja and Dashiell.

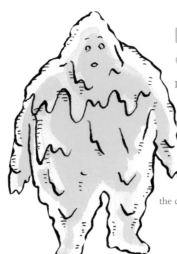

LEMONY SNICKET & RICHARD SALA 5

Lemony Snicket is the author of **A SERIES OF UNFORTUNATE EVENTS,** a sequence of supposedly fictional and allegedly beloved books chronicling the lives of the Baudelaire children. His whereabouts are currently unknown, although, recently, he was spotted near a cannery.

Since he was very young, Richard Sala has had a keen interest in musty old museums, narrow alleyways, hidden truths, double meanings, and late night walks. He lives in Berkeley, California, where he writes and draws the comic book series **EVIL EYE.**

J. OTTO SEIBOLD & VIVIAN WALSH 13

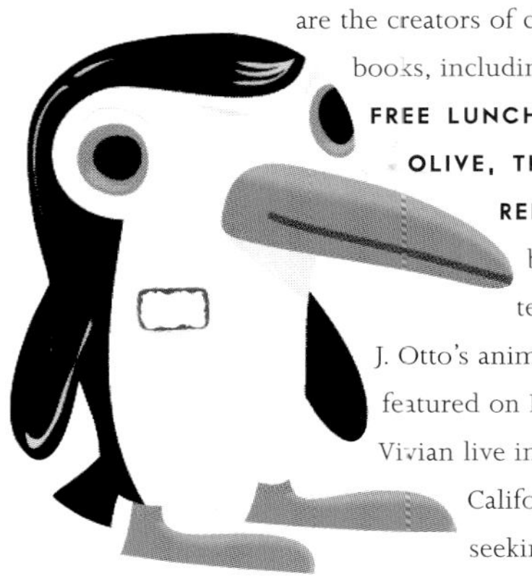

are the creators of children's books, including **GLUEY, FREE LUNCH,** and **OLIVE, THE OTHER REINDEER,** which became a one-hour television show.

J. Otto's animation has also been featured on MTV. J. Otto and Vivian live in San Francisco, California, where they are seeking their fortune and hope to live happily ever after.

TONY MILLIONAIRE 18

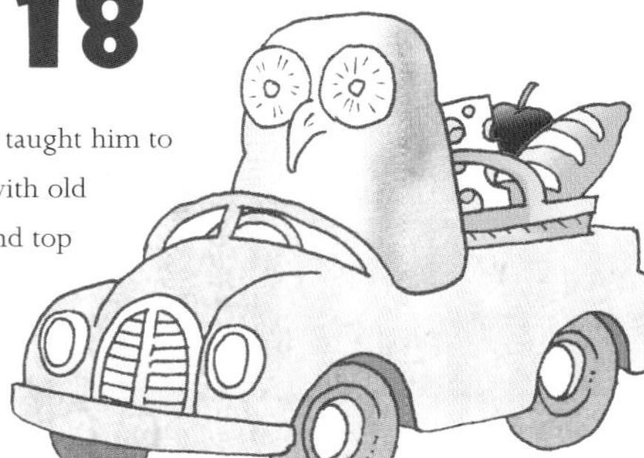

Tony Millionaire grew up in Massachusetts, where his grandparents taught him to draw ships and old houses. After spending his Sunday afternoons with old newspaper comics, he started drawing monkeys with striped tails and top hats. He now writes and draws **MAAKIES** and **SOCK MONKEY** in Pasadena, California, where he lives with his wife and daughter.

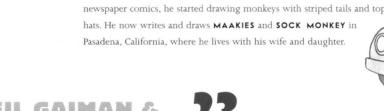

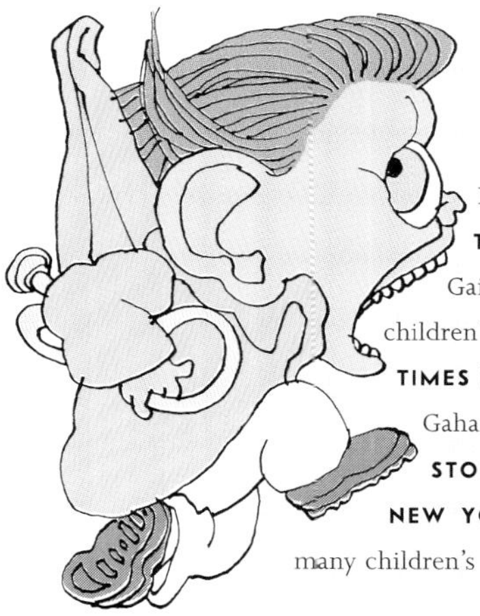

NEIL GAIMAN & GAHAN WILSON 23

Neil Gaiman is the creator/writer of the epic DC Comics fantasy series **THE SANDMAN** and has won every major award in the field. Recently, Gaiman won the Hugo Award for his novel **AMERICAN GODS,** and his children's novel, **CORALINE,** illustrated by Dave McKean, was a **NEW YORK TIMES** bestseller.

Gahan Wilson sold his first cartoon to a pulp magazine, **AMAZING STORIES,** in the early 50s. Since then his cartoons have appeared in **THE NEW YORKER** and **PLAYBOY,** among others. He has written and illustrated many children's books as well as produced over twenty anthologies of his cartoons.

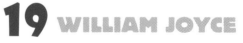

19 WILLIAM JOYCE

is the creator of numerous children's books, including **DINOSAUR BOB** and **GEORGE SHRINKS,** as well as the PBS television series **ROLIE POLIE OLIE** and **GEORGE SHRINKS.** He was born in Shreveport, Louisiana, where he now lives with his wife, their two children, and several psychotic animals. He is currently producing and designing a film about robots.

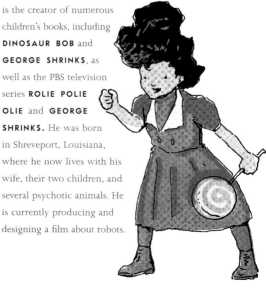

27 BASIL WOLVERTON

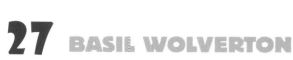

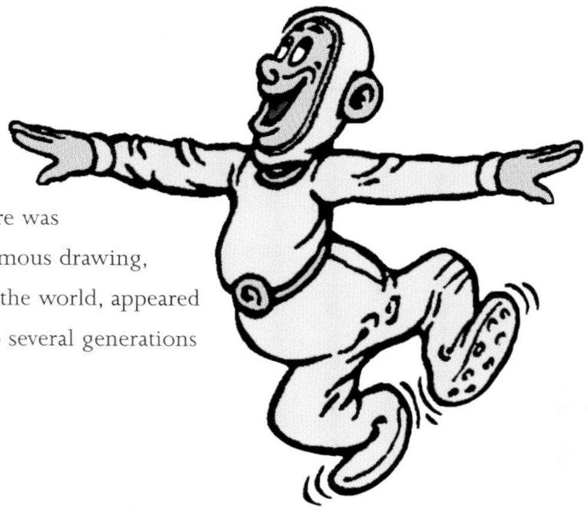

was born in 1909. Wolverton's first regular comics feature was **SPACEHAWKS** in **CIRCUS** comics in 1938. His most famous drawing, **"LENA THE HYENA,"** a depiction of the ugliest girl in the world, appeared in **LIFE** magazine in 1946. He has been an inspiration to several generations of cartoonists. He died in 1978.

EDITED BY
A RAW Junior Book

ND SILLY NIGHT...

31 JOOST SWARTE

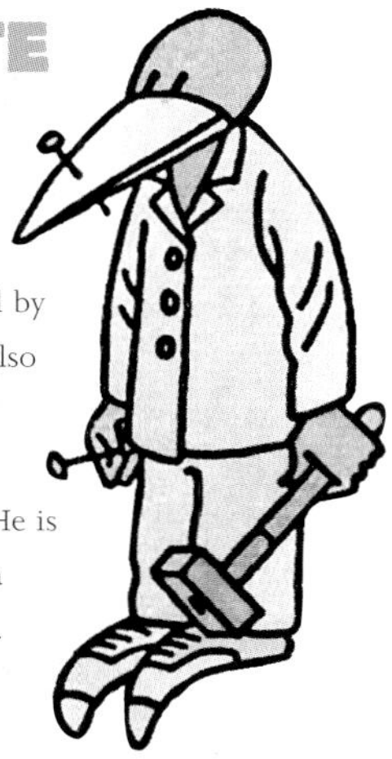

Among Joost's many past projects are a series of comics for children and postage stamps officially issued by the Dutch post office. He has also designed a theater, just built and opened in his hometown of Haarlem, The Netherlands. He is married, has three daughters; a grandson, Buster; and two cats.

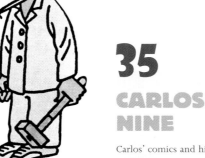

35 CARLOS NINE

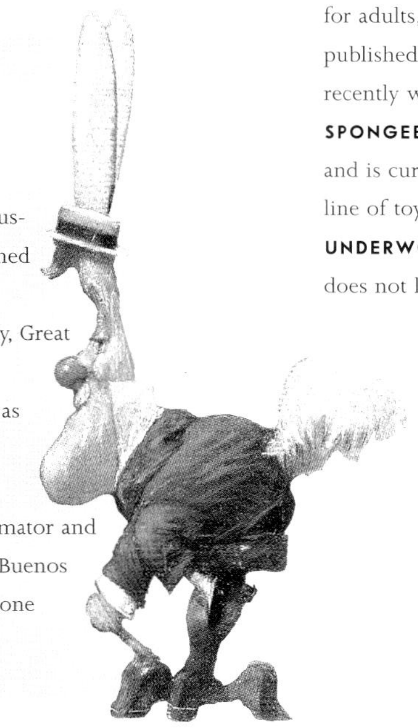

Carlos' comics and his illustrations have been published in the U.S., Spain, Italy, France, Belgium, Germany, Great Britain, Mexico, Brazil, Taiwan, and Hong Kong, as well as in his native Argentina. He's also a painter, a sculptor, an animator and a playwright. He lives in Buenos Aires with his three cats, one turtle and four children.

KAZ 39

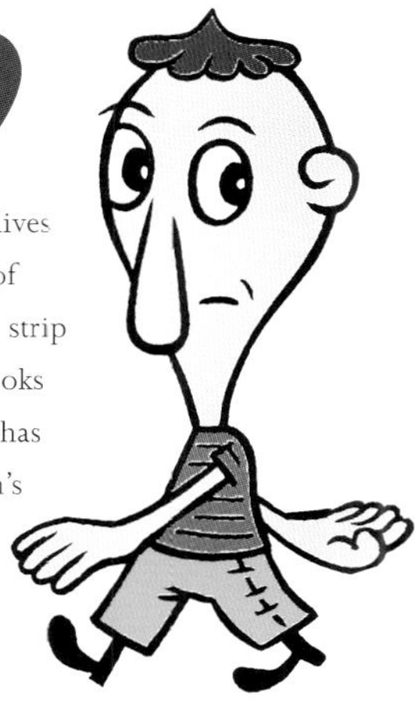

KAZ was born in Hoboken, New Jersey, and now lives in Manhattan. He is the creator of **UNDERWORLD,** a weekly comic strip for adults, collected into four books published by Fantagraphics. Kaz has recently written for Nickelodeon's **SPONGEBOB SQUAREPANTS** and is currently working on a line of toys based on his **UNDERWORLD** characters. He does not like wearing gloves on his head either.

BARBARA McCLINTOCK 43

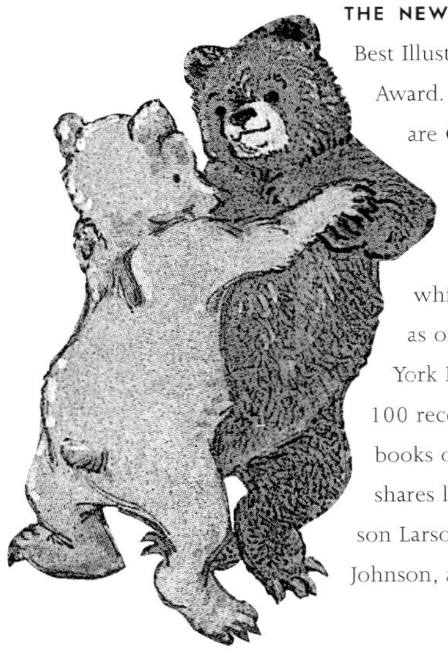

Three of Barbara's many books have won **THE NEW YORK TIMES** Best Illustrated Books Award. Among her latest are **GOLDILOCKS AND THE THREE BEARS** and **DAHLIA,** which was selected as one of the New York Public Library's 100 recommended books of 2002. She shares life and love with son Larson, fiancé David Johnson, and two cats.

44 PATRICK McDONNELL

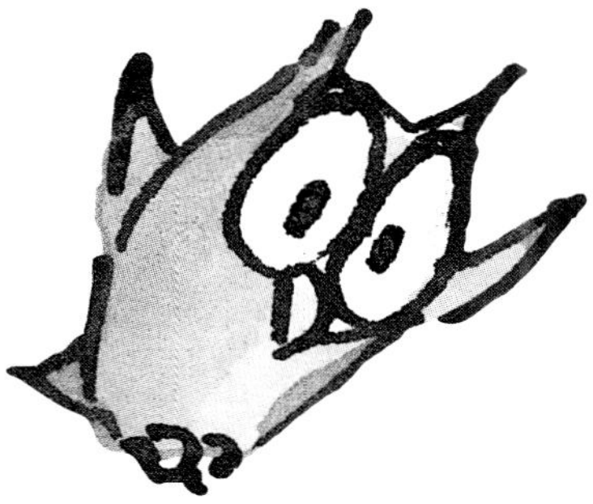

created the comic strip **MUTTS** in 1994. The **MUTTS** characters now appear in over 500 newspapers, in 10 book collections and a new coffee-table book, **MUTTS, THE COMIC ART OF PATRICK McDONNELL,** as well as on a New Jersey license plate (Patrick's home state). He lives there with his wife, Karen; his dog, Earl; and his cat, Meemow.

48 R. SIKORYAK

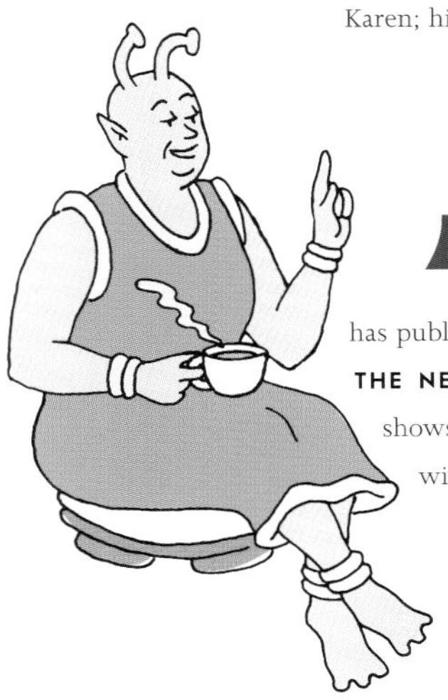

has published cartoons and illustrations in **NICKELODEON MAGAZINE, THE NEW YORKER,** and many others. In his spare time, he creates slide shows for Off-Off Broadway theater. He lives in Manhattan with his wife, Kriota, and their two cats.

MARTIN HANDFORD

is the author of the popular **WHERE'S WALDO?** series of books. He was born in Hampstead, England, where he lives with his wife, Elizabeth, and their two children.

LOOK HERE: ONE MORE GAME!

Look carefully at each one of the drawings on these two pages, then turn to the endpapers in the front and in the back of the book. Each drawing is hidden (somewhere) in the endpapers.

CAN YOU FIND THEM ALL?

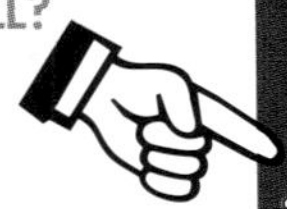

ENDPAPERS

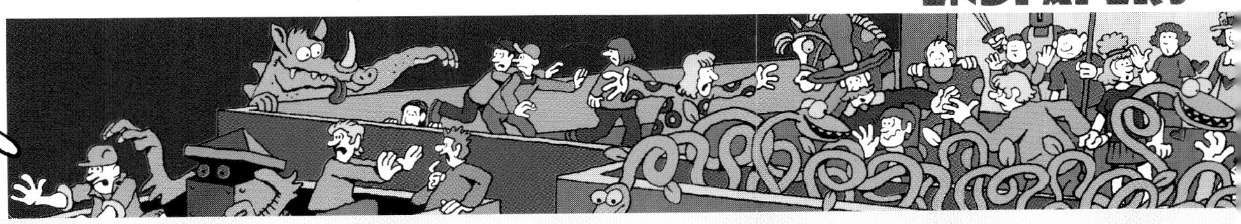

ART SPIEGELMAN & FRANÇOISE MOULY
with JOANNA COTLER BOOKS/an imprint of HarperCollins*Publishers*

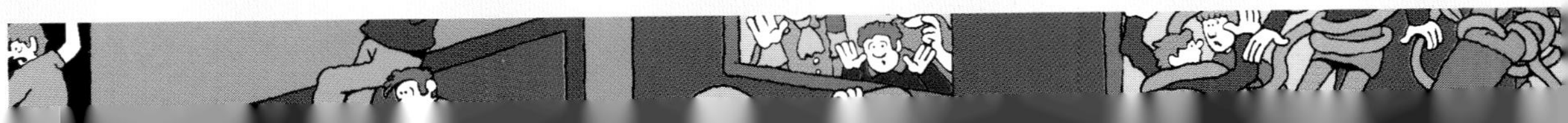

dedicated to DASHIELL and NADJA

designed by FRANÇOISE MOULY

editorial assistant:
ISAAC RAMOS

production advisor:
GREG CAPTAIN

production:
FRANÇOISE MOULY
BARBARA KOPELOFF
ANDREW DEUTSCH
NOVA REN SUMA

with grateful thanks to:
GREG CAPTAIN
LEE HEYDOLPH
JOSEPH PALMERI
JANICE YU

For information write to HarperCollins Children's Books, a division of HarperCollins Publishers Inc., 1350 Avenue of the Americas, New York, NY 10019. www.harperchildrens.com. Library of Congress Cataloging-in-Publication Data: LITTLE LIT: It Was a Dark and Silly Night.../edited by Art Spiegelman & Françoise Mouly. p.cm.— (Little Lit ;3) "Comics by Lemony Snicket, William Joyce, Neil Gaiman, and more!" ISBN 0-06-028628-8 1. Comic books, strips, etc. —United States. I. Spiegelman, Art. II. Mouly, Françoise. III Series. PN6726.I43 2003 741.5 ' 973—dc21 2003042307
Printed in Malaysia
10 9 8
7 6 5
4 3
2
1

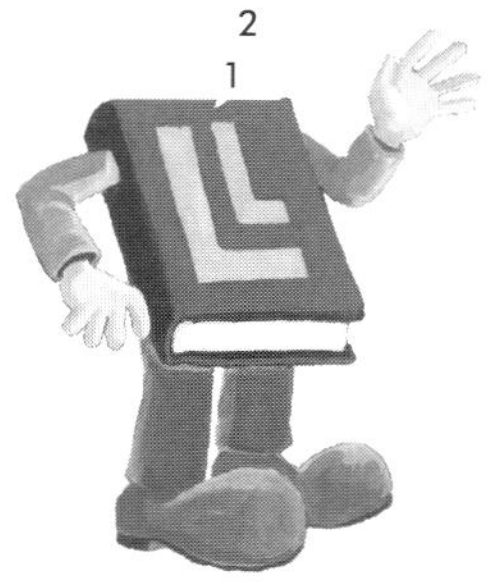

Visit us at www.little-lit.com

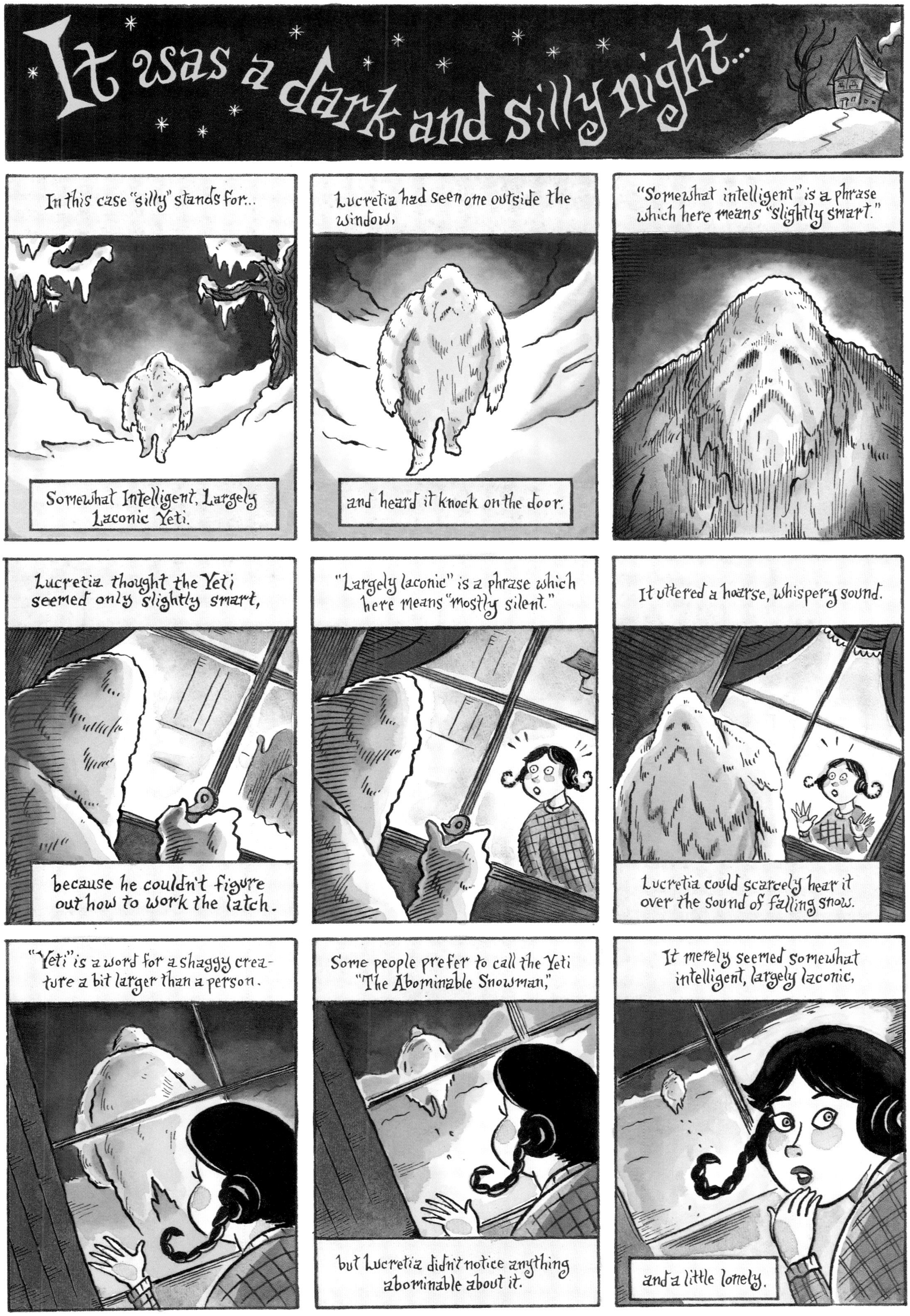
It was a dark and silly night...
In this case "silly" stands for...
Somewhat Intelligent, Largely Laconic Yeti.
Lucretia had seen one outside the window,
and heard it knock on the door.
"Somewhat intelligent" is a phrase which here means "slightly smart."
Lucretia thought the Yeti seemed only slightly smart,
because he couldn't figure out how to work the latch.
"Largely laconic" is a phrase which here means "mostly silent."
It uttered a hoarse, whispery sound.
Lucretia could scarcely hear it over the sound of falling snow.
"Yeti" is a word for a shaggy creature a bit larger than a person.
Some people prefer to call the Yeti "The Abominable Snowman,"
but Lucretia didn't notice anything abominable about it.
It merely seemed somewhat intelligent, largely laconic,
and a little lonely.

Lucretia was a little lonely herself. She lived in a small village so high up in the mountains that it was winter every day of the year.

In the daytime, she went to snow school.

If Bill has two snowflakes, and Elsie has three snowflakes...

In the nighttime, she sat with her mother and her father and her baby brother, ate toast, and stared out the window.

Listen to the wind blow!

The Yeti was the first exciting thing that had happened to her in three and a half years.

I just saw a Yeti outside the window.

Nonsense!

It was somewhat intelligent, and largely laconic.

Don't be absurd!

I think it knocked on the door.

That was the wind! There is no such thing as a Yeti.

I'd prefer to find out for myself.

We don't always get what we prefer, Lucretia.

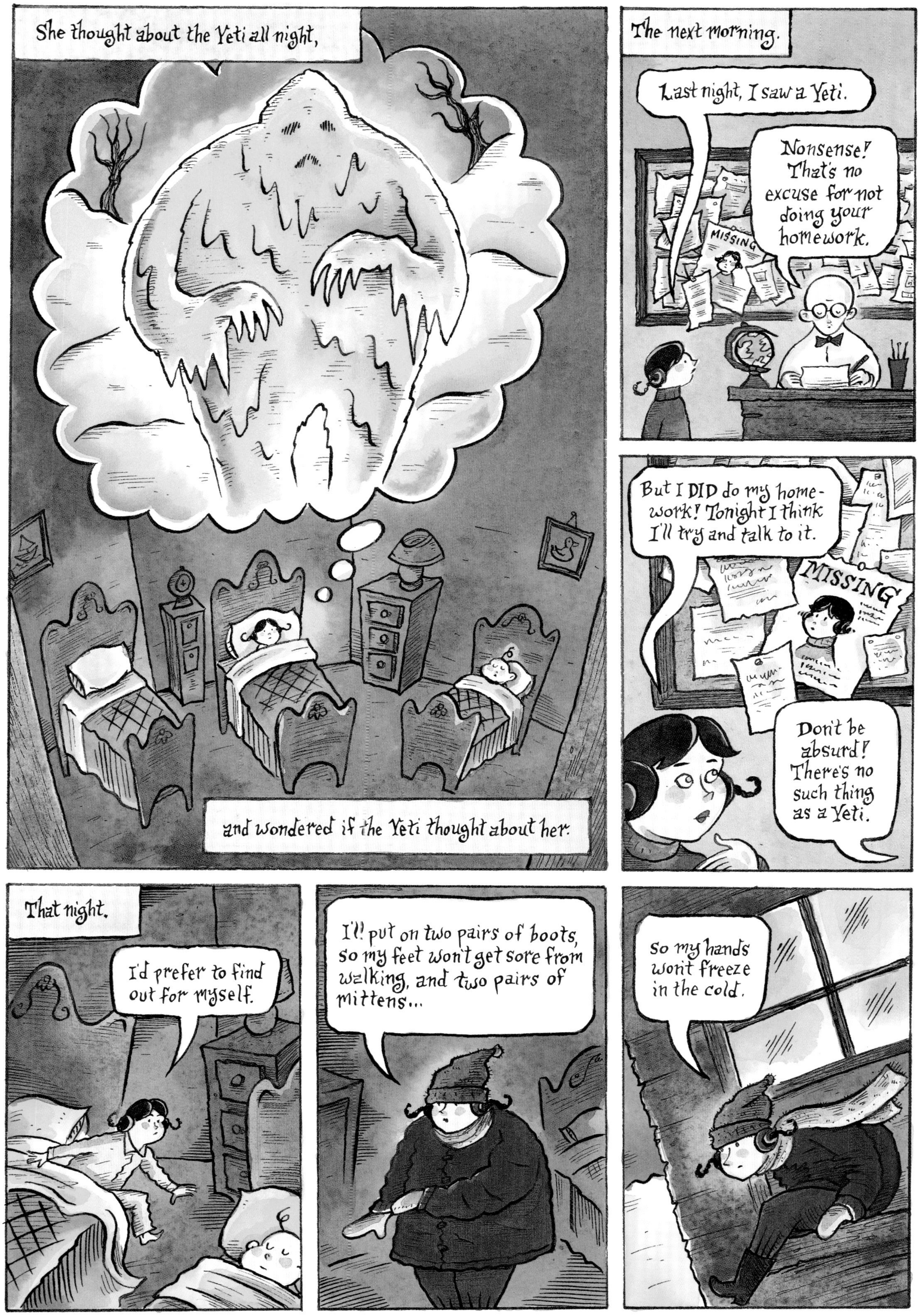
She thought about the Yeti all night,
and wondered if the Yeti thought about her.
The next morning.
Last night, I saw a Yeti.
Nonsense! That's no excuse for not doing your homework.
MISSING
But I DID do my home-work! Tonight I think I'll try and talk to it.
MISSING
Don't be absurd! There's no such thing as a Yeti.
That night.
I'd prefer to find out for myself.
I'll put on two pairs of boots, so my feet won't get sore from walking, and two pairs of mittens...
So my hands won't freeze in the cold.

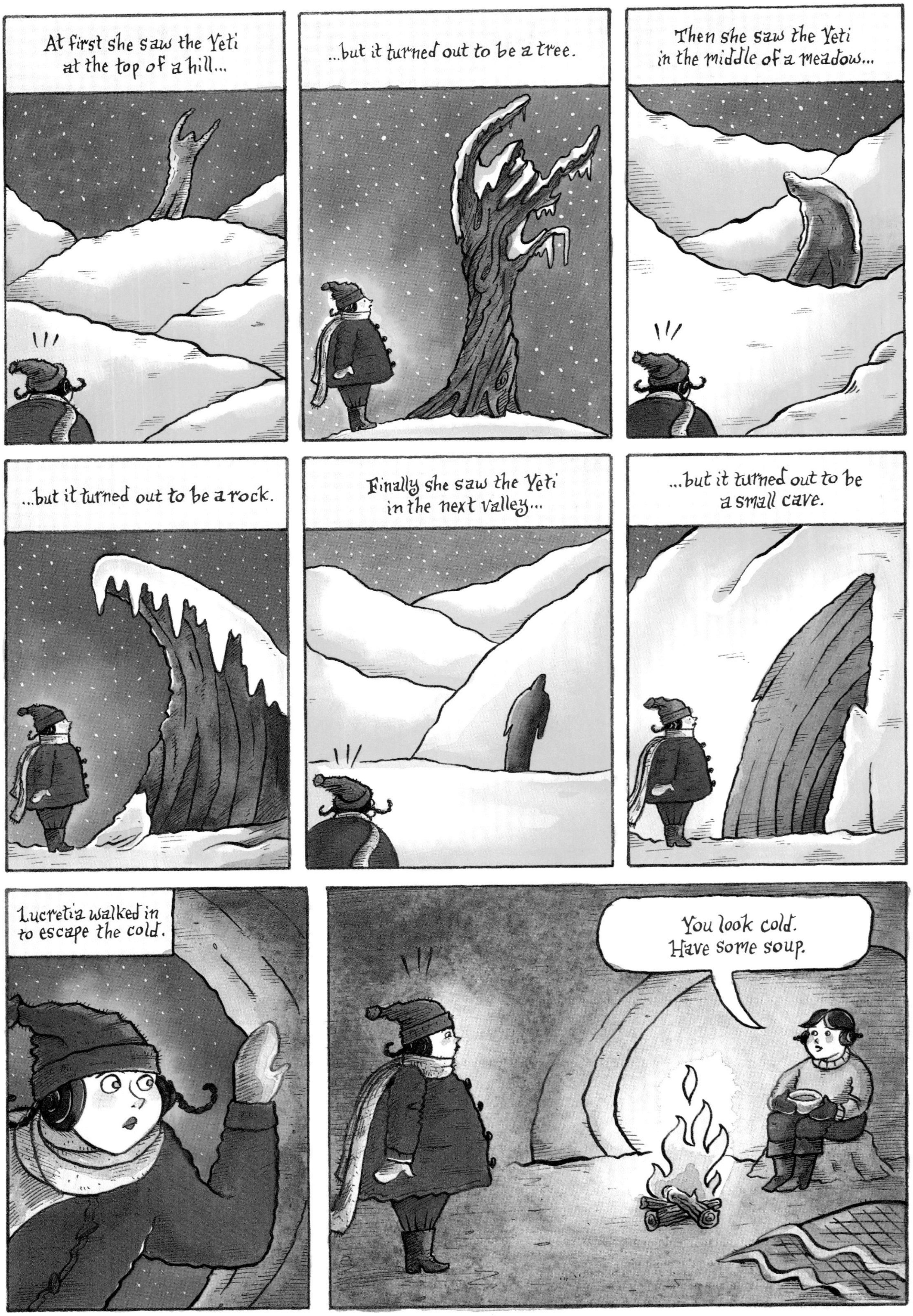
At first she saw the Yeti at the top of a hill...
...but it turned out to be a tree.
Then she saw the Yeti in the middle of a meadow...
...but it turned out to be a rock.
Finally she saw the Yeti in the next valley...
...but it turned out to be a small cave.
Lucretia walked in to escape the cold.
You look cold. Have some soup.

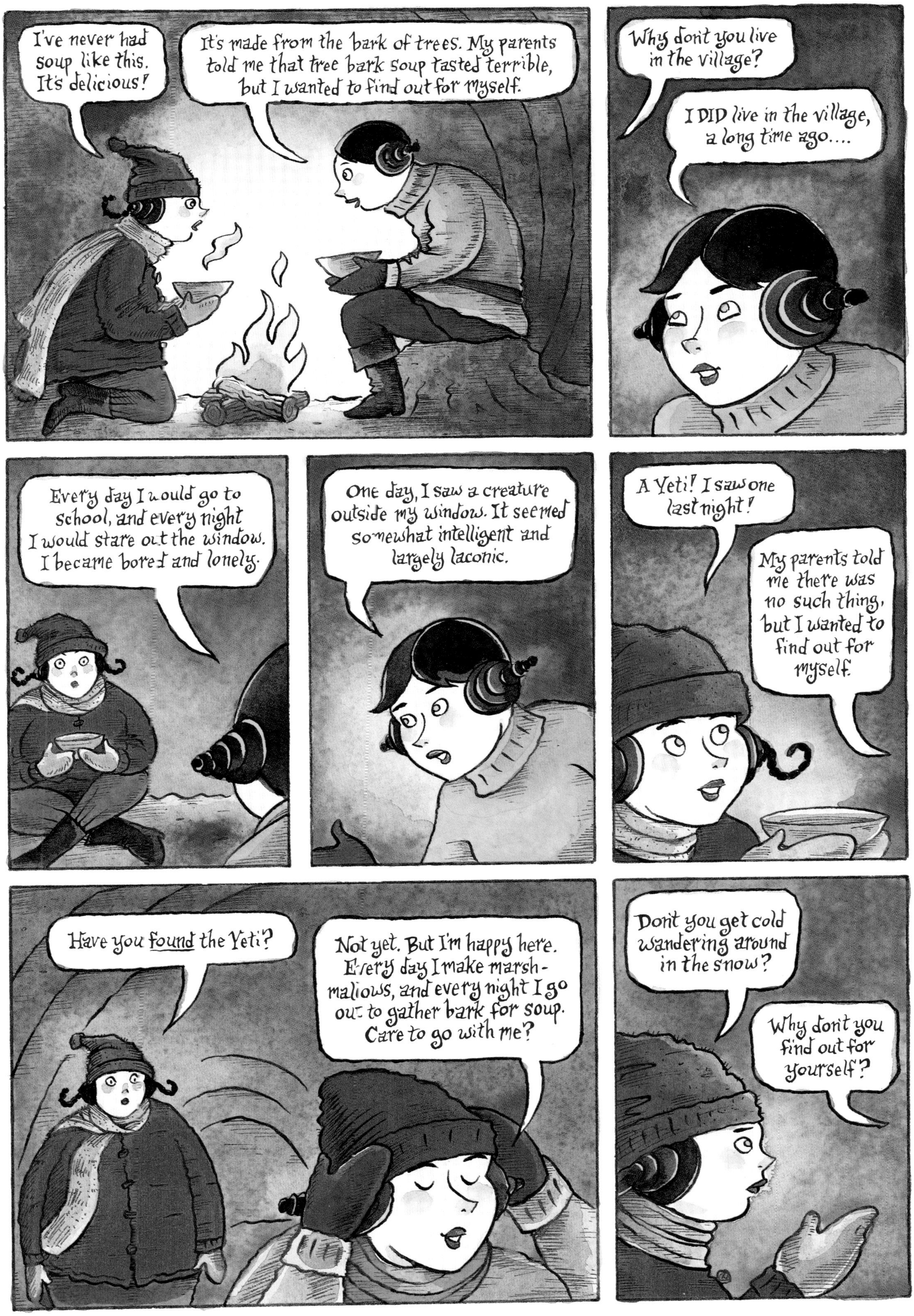
I've never had soup like this. It's delicious!
It's made from the bark of trees. My parents told me that tree bark soup tasted terrible, but I wanted to find out for myself.
Why don't you live in the village?
I DID live in the village, a long time ago....
Every day I would go to school, and every night I would stare out the window. I became bored and lonely.
One day, I saw a creature outside my window. It seemed somewhat intelligent and largely laconic.
A Yeti! I saw one last night!
My parents told me there was no such thing, but I wanted to find out for myself.
Have you found the Yeti?
Not yet. But I'm happy here. Every day I make marsh-mallows, and every night I go out to gather bark for soup. Care to go with me?
Don't you get cold wandering around in the snow?
Why don't you find out for yourself?

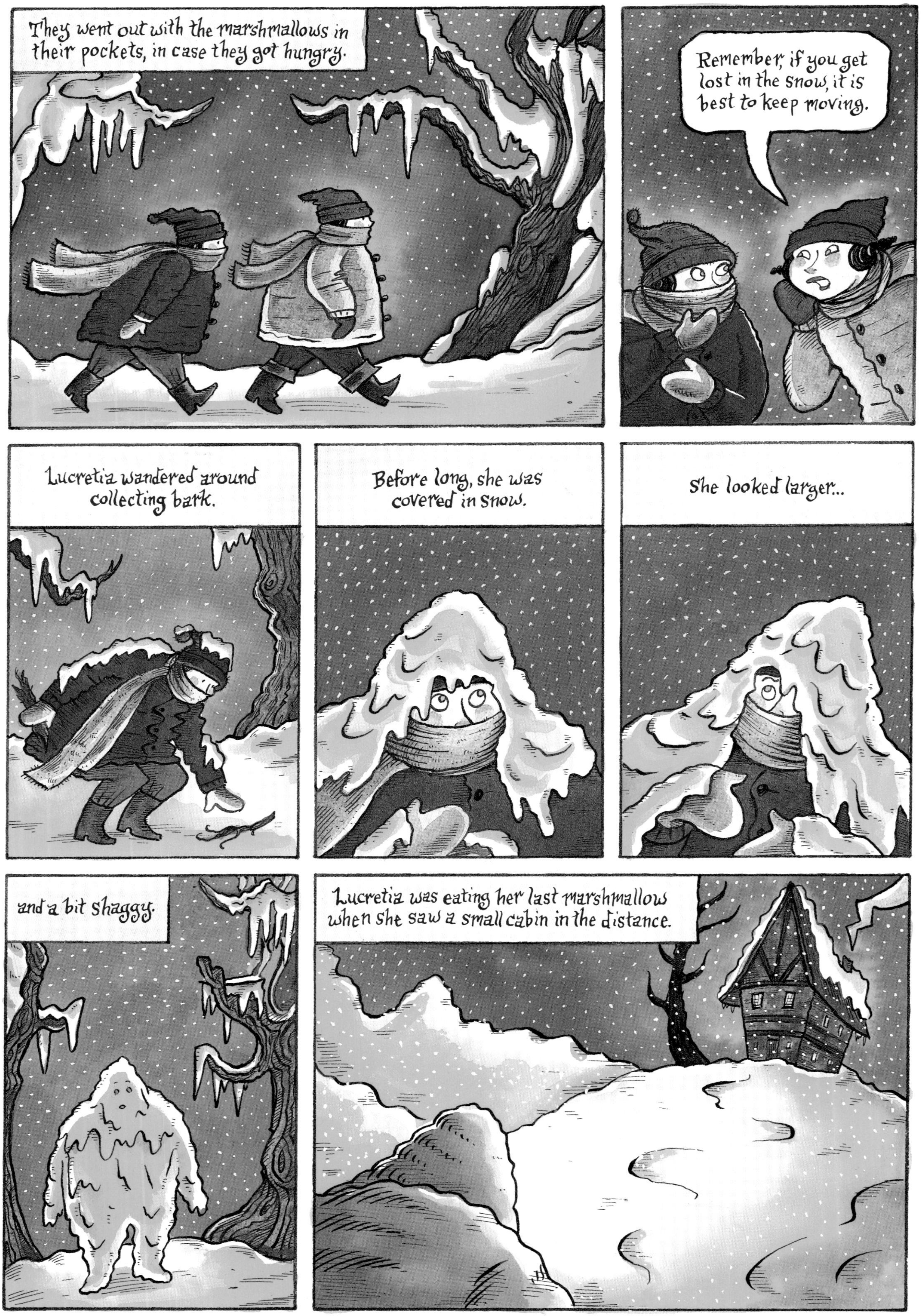
They went out with the marshmallows in their pockets, in case they got hungry.
Remember, if you get lost in the snow, it is best to keep moving.
Lucretia wandered around collecting bark.
Before long, she was covered in snow.
She looked larger...
and a bit shaggy.
Lucretia was eating her last marshmallow when she saw a small cabin in the distance.

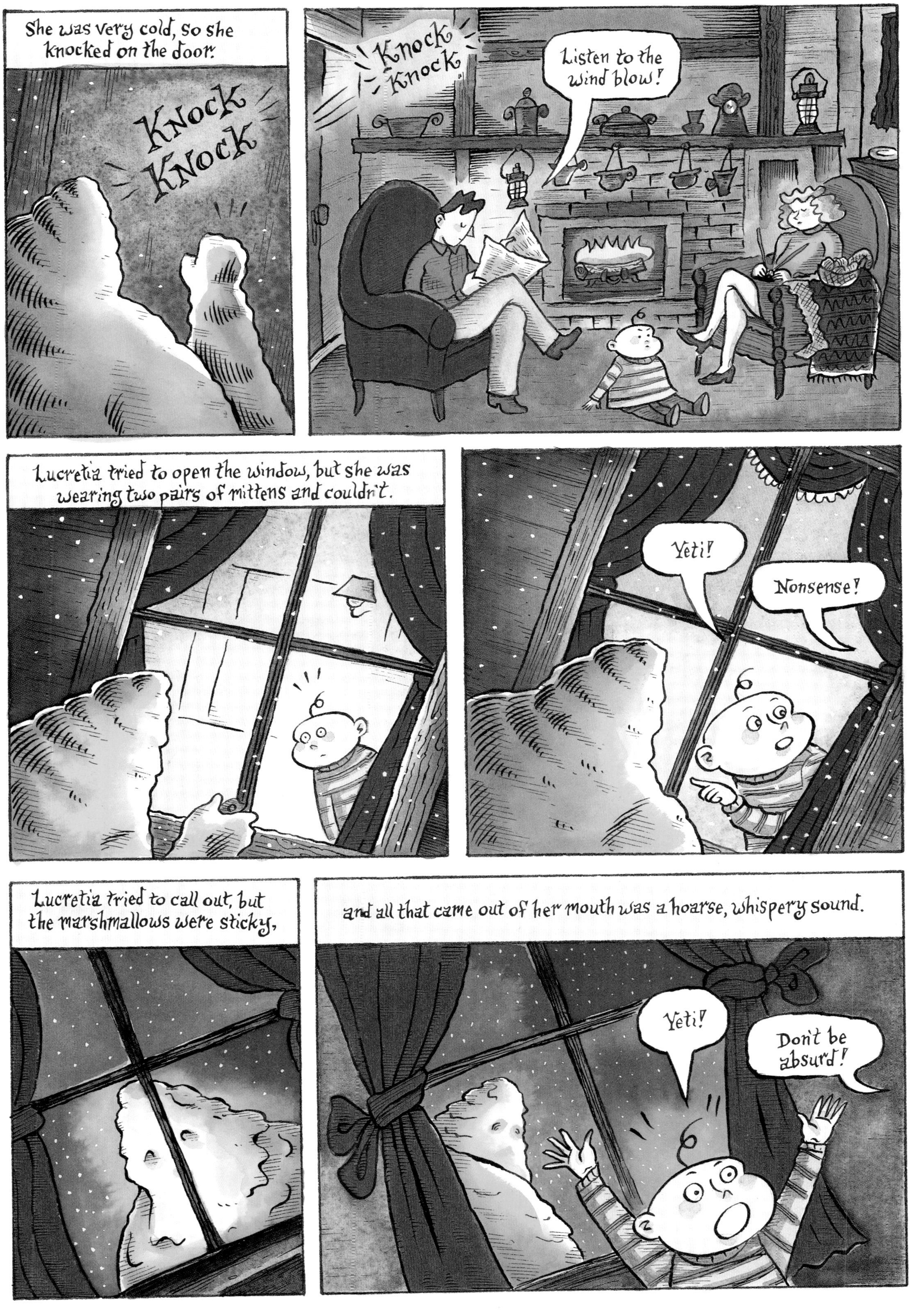
She was very cold, so she knocked on the door.
KNOCK KNOCK
Knock Knock
Listen to the wind blow!
Lucretia tried to open the window, but she was wearing two pairs of mittens and couldn't.
Yeti!
Nonsense!
Lucretia tried to call out, but the marshmallows were sticky,
and all that came out of her mouth was a hoarse, whispery sound.
Yeti!
Don't be absurd!

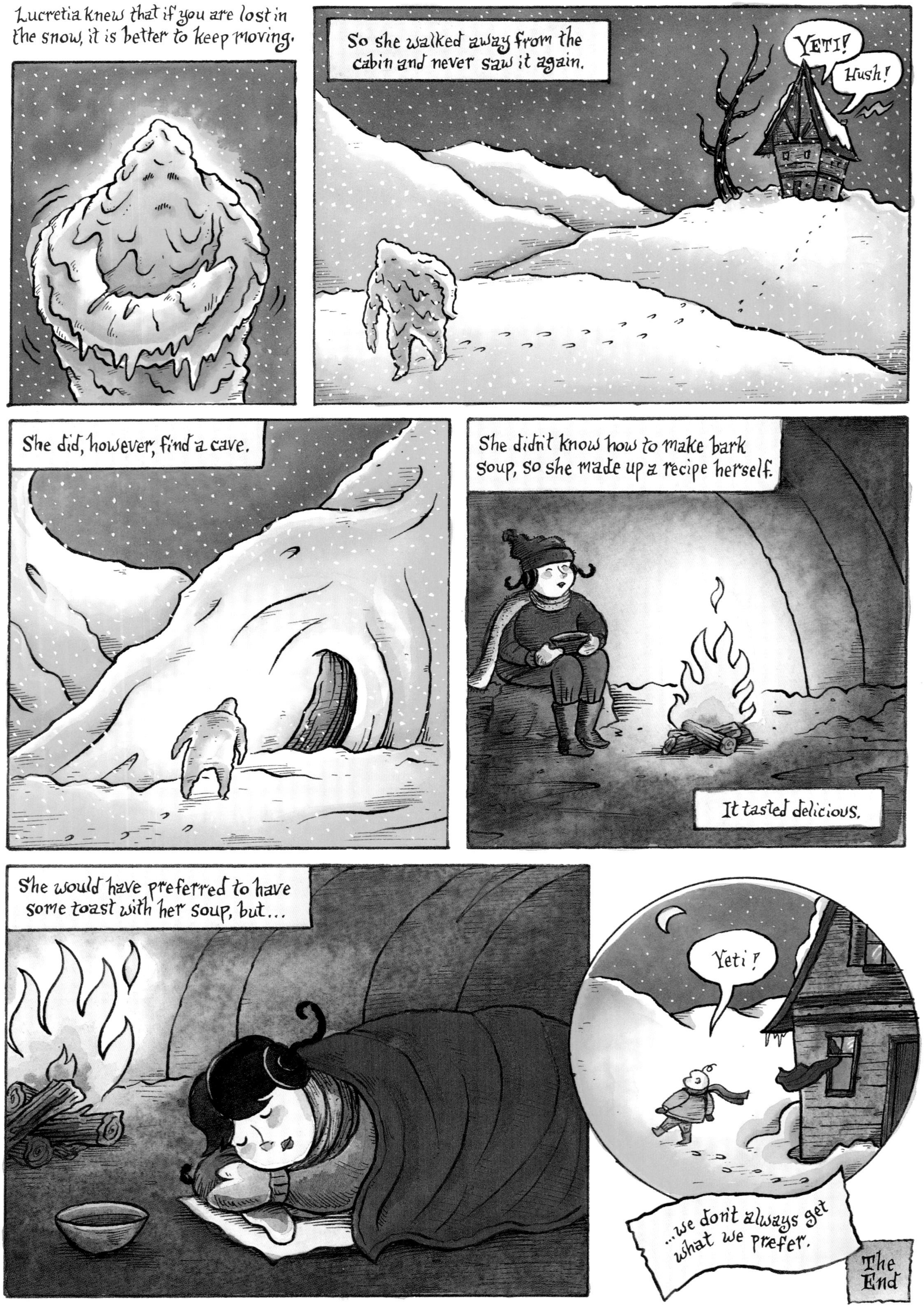
Lucretia knew that if you are lost in the snow, it is better to keep moving.
So she walked away from the cabin and never saw it again.
YETI!
Hush!
She did, however, find a cave.
She didn't know how to make bark soup, so she made up a recipe herself.
It tasted delicious.
She would have preferred to have some toast with her soup, but...
Yeti!
...we don't always get what we prefer.
The End

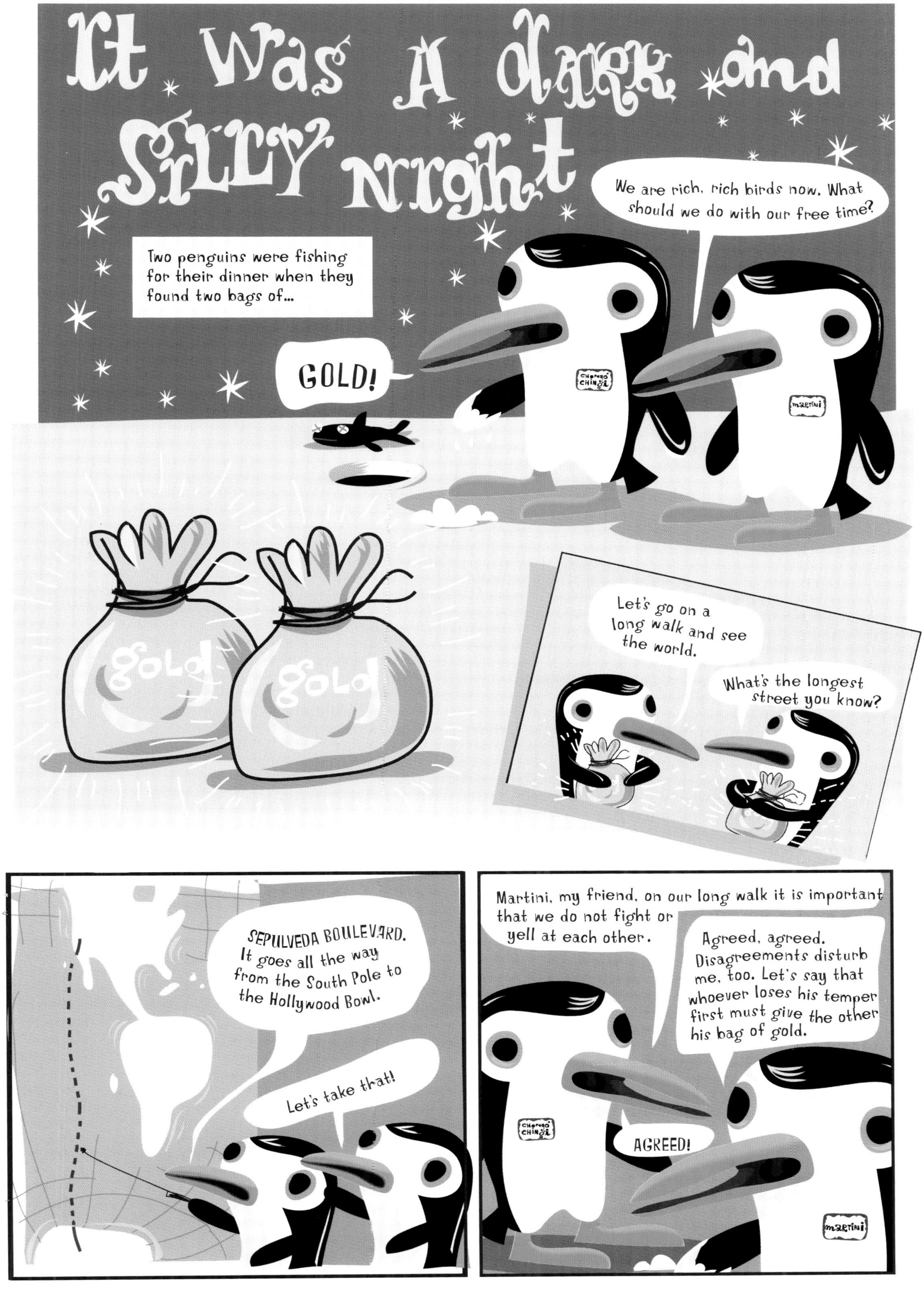
It Was A dark and Silly night
Two penguins were fishing for their dinner when they found two bags of...
GOLD!
We are rich, rich birds now. What should we do with our free time?
gold
gold
Let's go on a long walk and see the world.
What's the longest street you know?
SEPULVEDA BOULEVARD. It goes all the way from the South Pole to the Hollywood Bowl.
Let's take that!
Martini, my friend, on our long walk it is important that we do not fight or yell at each other.
Agreed, agreed. Disagreements disturb me, too. Let's say that whoever loses his temper first must give the other his bag of gold.
AGREED!
martini

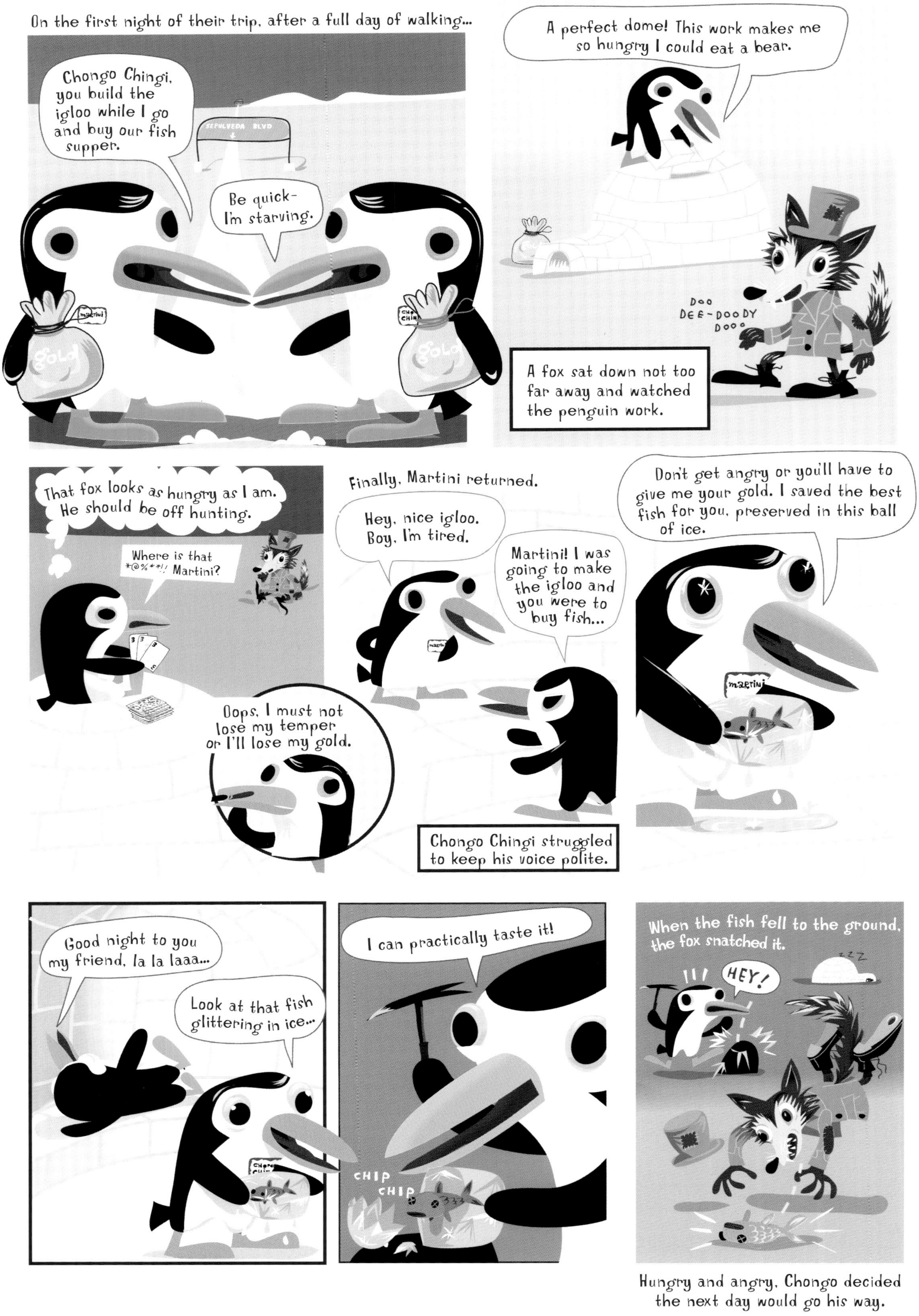
On the first night of their trip, after a full day of walking...
Chongo Chingi, you build the igloo while I go and buy our fish supper.
SEPULVEDA BLVD
Be quick–I'm starving.
GOLD
GOLD
A perfect dome! This work makes me so hungry I could eat a bear.
DOO DEE-DOODY DOOO
A fox sat down not too far away and watched the penguin work.
That fox looks as hungry as I am. He should be off hunting.
Where is that *@%**!! Martini?
Finally, Martini returned.
Hey, nice igloo. Boy, I'm tired.
Martini! I was going to make the igloo and you were to buy fish...
Oops, I must not lose my temper or I'll lose my gold.
Chongo Chingi struggled to keep his voice polite.
Don't get angry or you'll have to give me your gold. I saved the best fish for you, preserved in this ball of ice.
martini
Good night to you my friend, la la laaa...
Look at that fish glittering in ice...
I can practically taste it!
CHIP
CHIP
When the fish fell to the ground, the fox snatched it.
HEY!
Hungry and angry, Chongo decided the next day would go his way.

The next afternoon, the two penguins strolled into Hollywood.

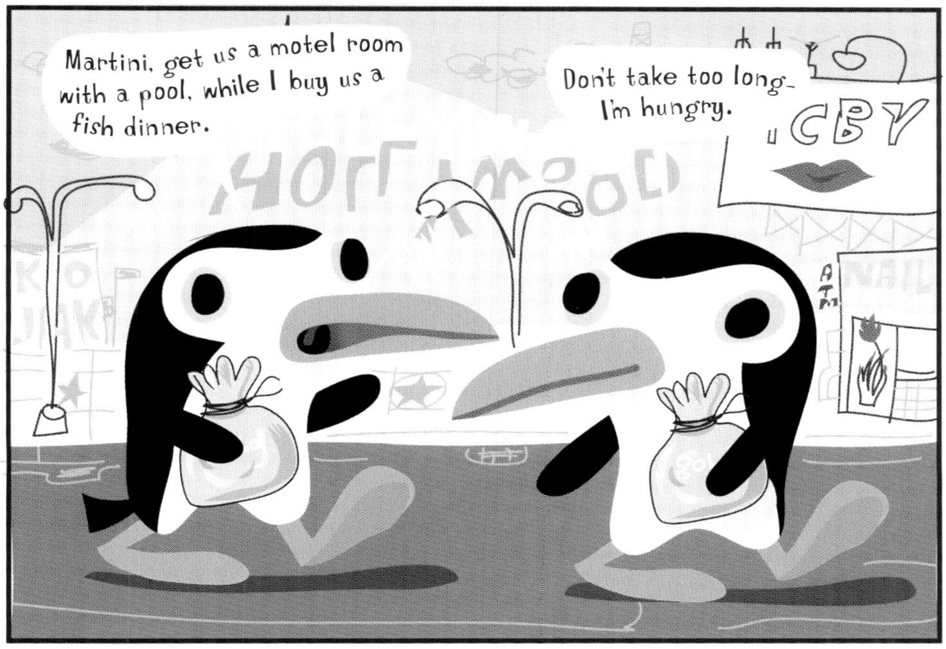
Martini, get us a motel room with a pool, while I buy us a fish dinner.
Don't take too long-I'm hungry.

Martini found a nice motel and started waiting...

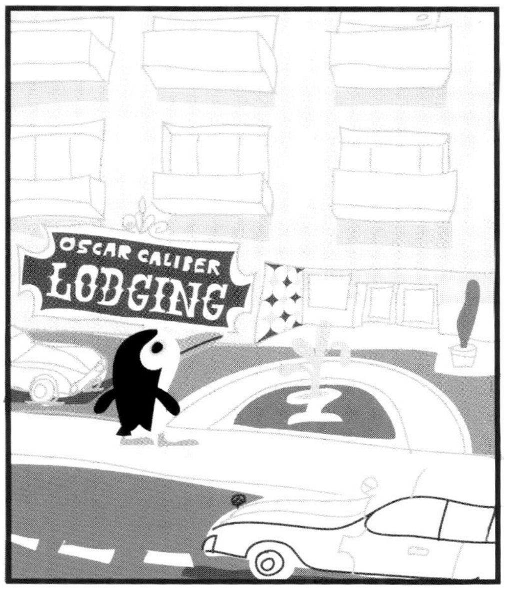
OSCAR CALIBER
LODGING

...and waiting.

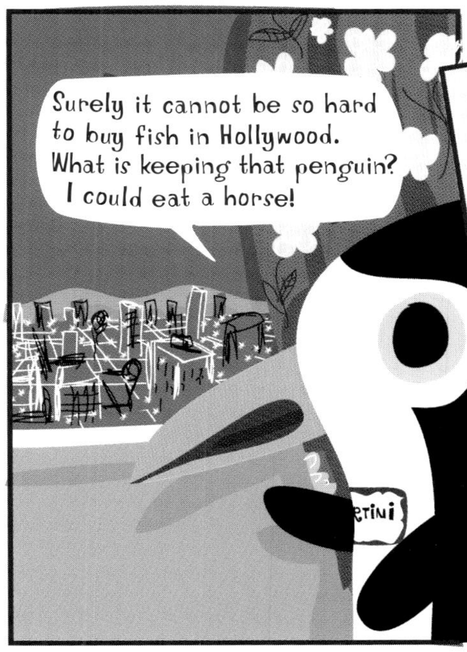
Surely it cannot be so hard to buy fish in Hollywood. What is keeping that penguin? I could eat a horse!

When suddenly...

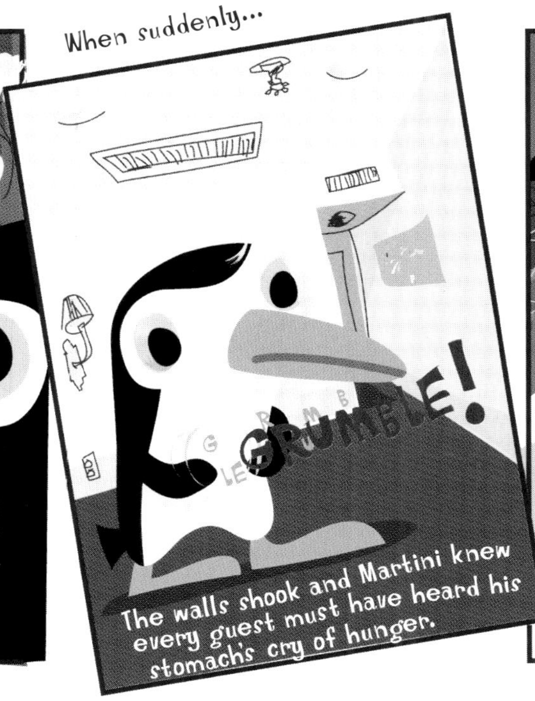
GRUMBLE!
The walls shook and Martini knew every guest must have heard his stomach's cry of hunger.

Sure enough, on the balcony facing Martini's, a fox appeared.

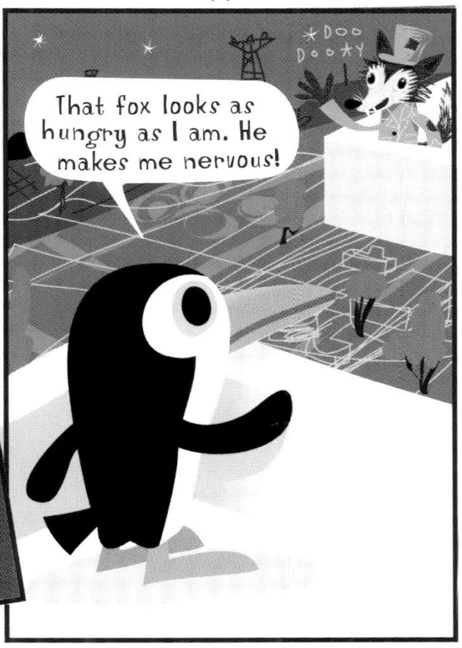
That fox looks as hungry as I am. He makes me nervous!

He pulled the curtains to escape the fox's watchful eyes.

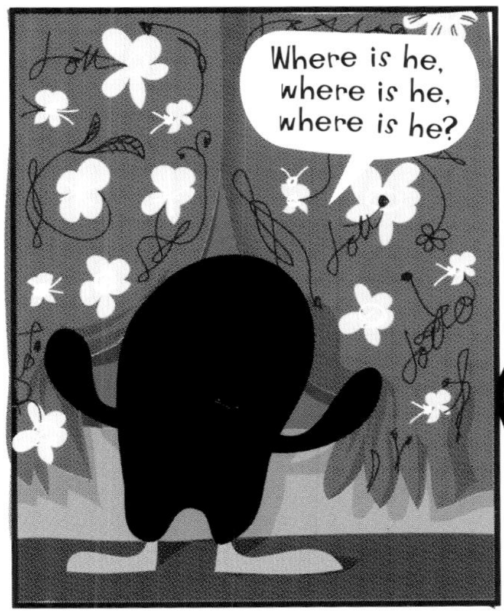
Where is he, where is he, where is he?

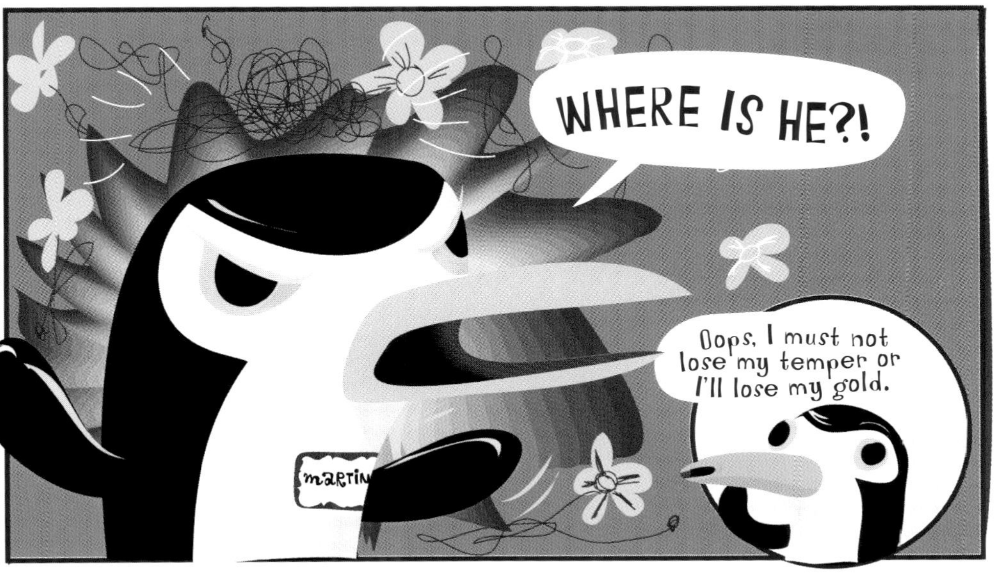
WHERE IS HE?!
Oops, I must not lose my temper or I'll lose my gold.
MARTINI

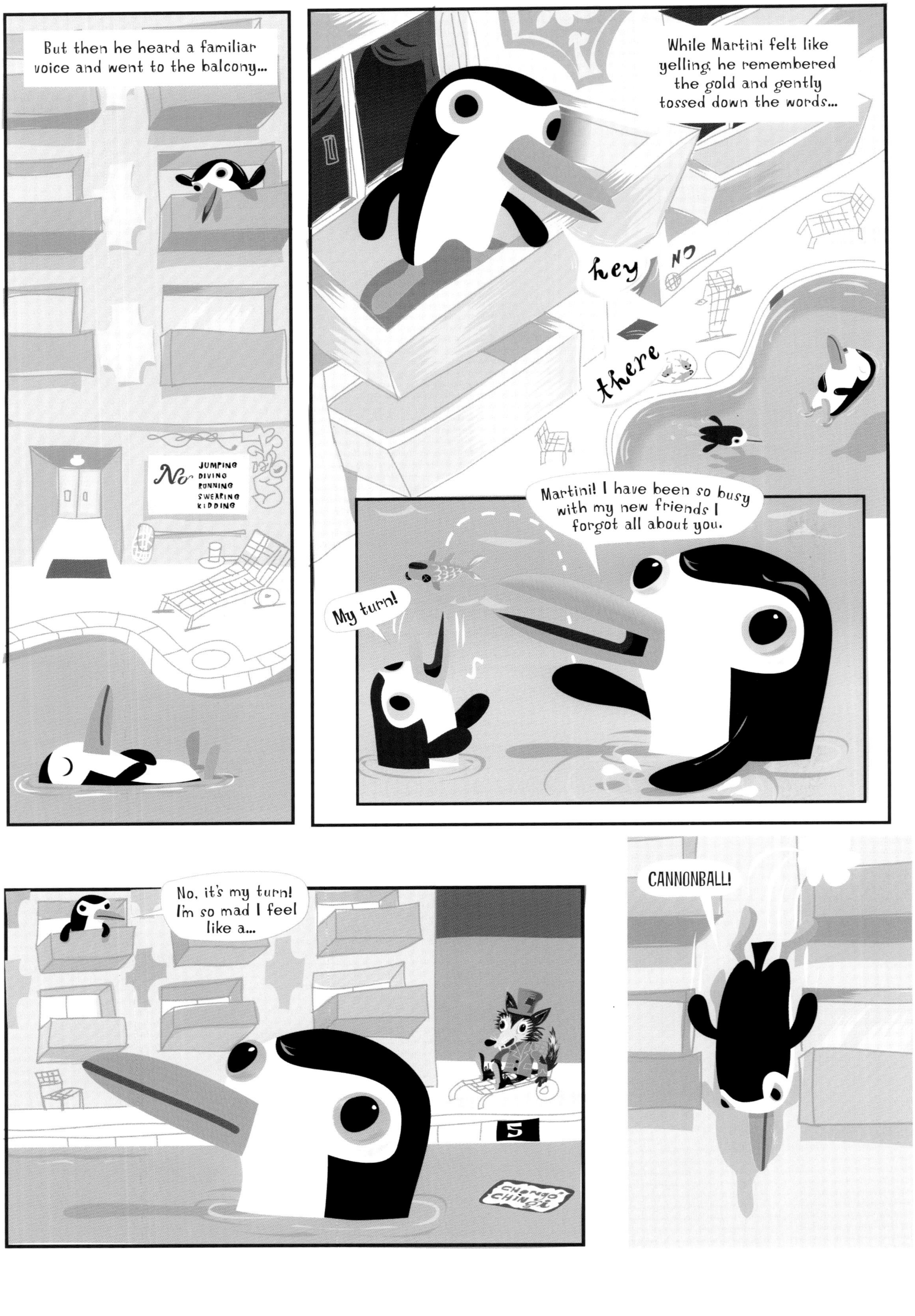
But then he heard a familiar voice and went to the balcony...
No JUMPING DIVING RUNNING SWEARING KIDDING
While Martini felt like yelling, he remembered the gold and gently tossed down the words...
hey
NO
there
Martini! I have been so busy with my new friends I forgot all about you.
My turn!
No, it's my turn! I'm so mad I feel like a...
5
CANNONBALL!

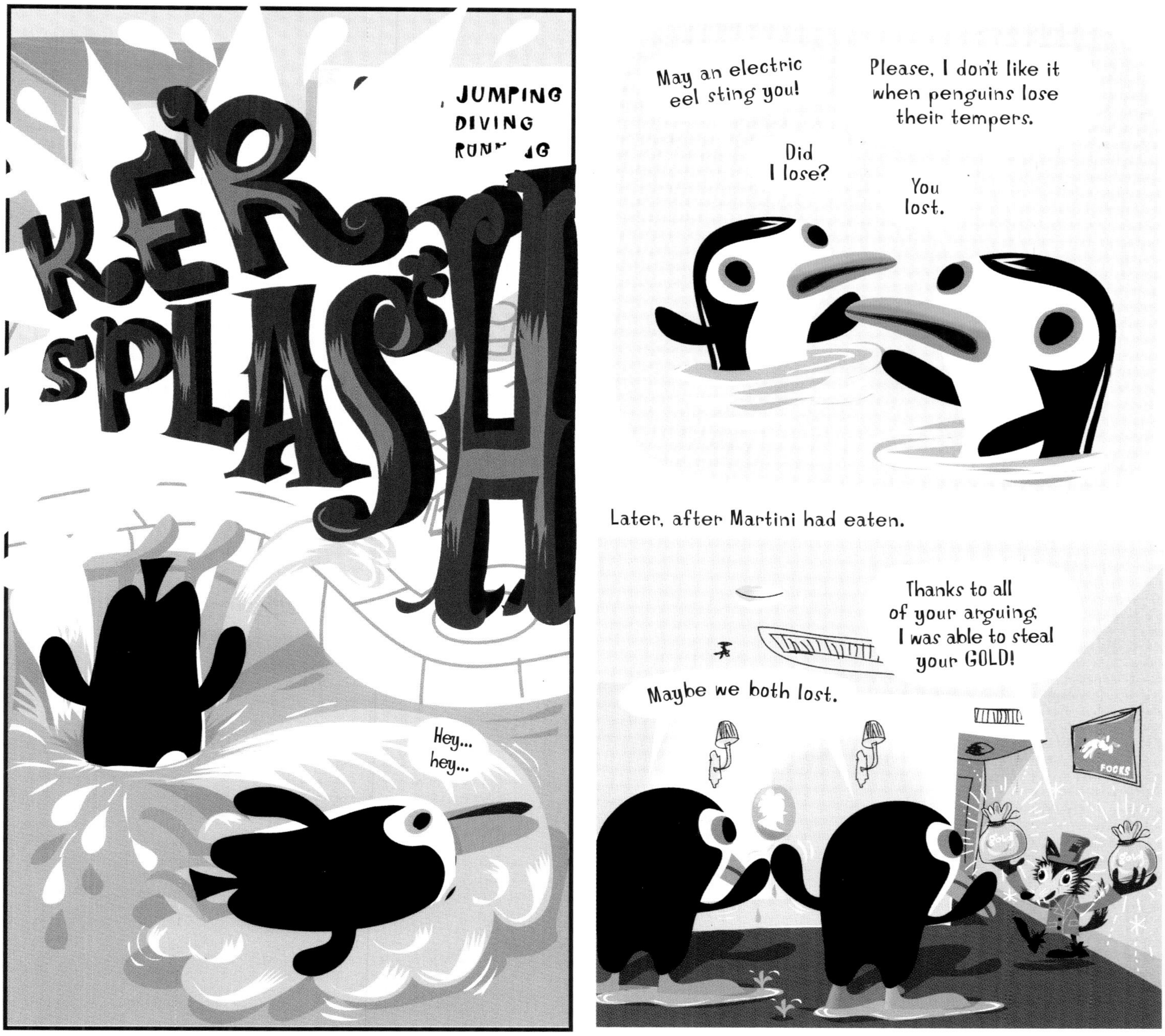
JUMPING
DIVING
KER SPLASH
Hey... hey...
May an electric eel sting you!
Please, I don't like it when penguins lose their tempers.
Did I lose?
You lost.
Later, after Martini had eaten.
Thanks to all of your arguing, I was able to steal your GOLD!
Maybe we both lost.
GOLD
GOLD
FOCKS

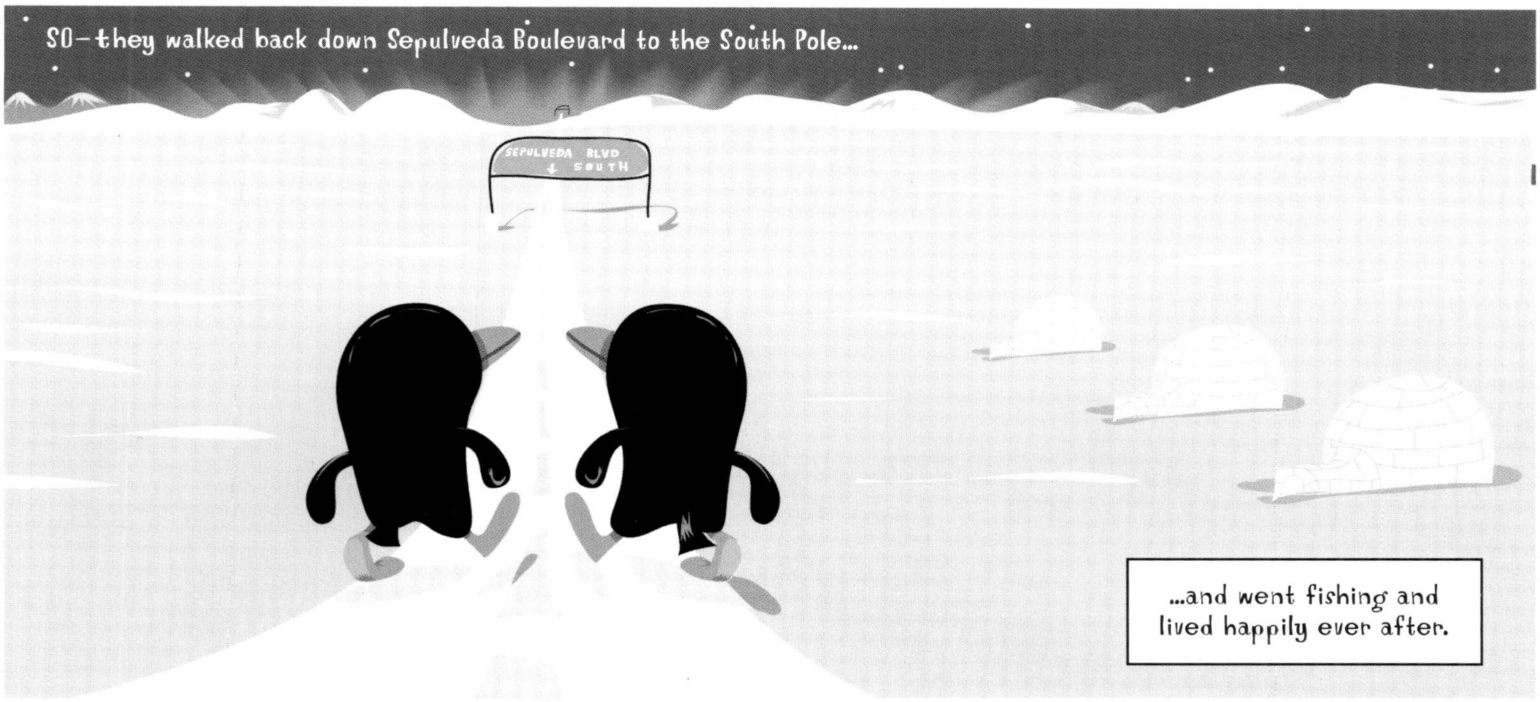
SO—they walked back down Sepulveda Boulevard to the South Pole...
SEPULVEDA BLVD
↓ SOUTH
...and went fishing and lived happily ever after.

tony millionaire

IT WAS A DARK AND SILLY NIGHT...

...AND AFTER A LONG DAY'S SLEEP, THE OWL GOT INTO HIS CAR AND WENT SHOPPING. THIS IS A COMIC STRIP ABOUT HIS SHOPPING TRIP, BUT SOMEHOW THE CARTOONIST MIXED UP THE PANELS! CAN YOU REARRANGE THEM SO THAT THE STORY MAKES SENSE?

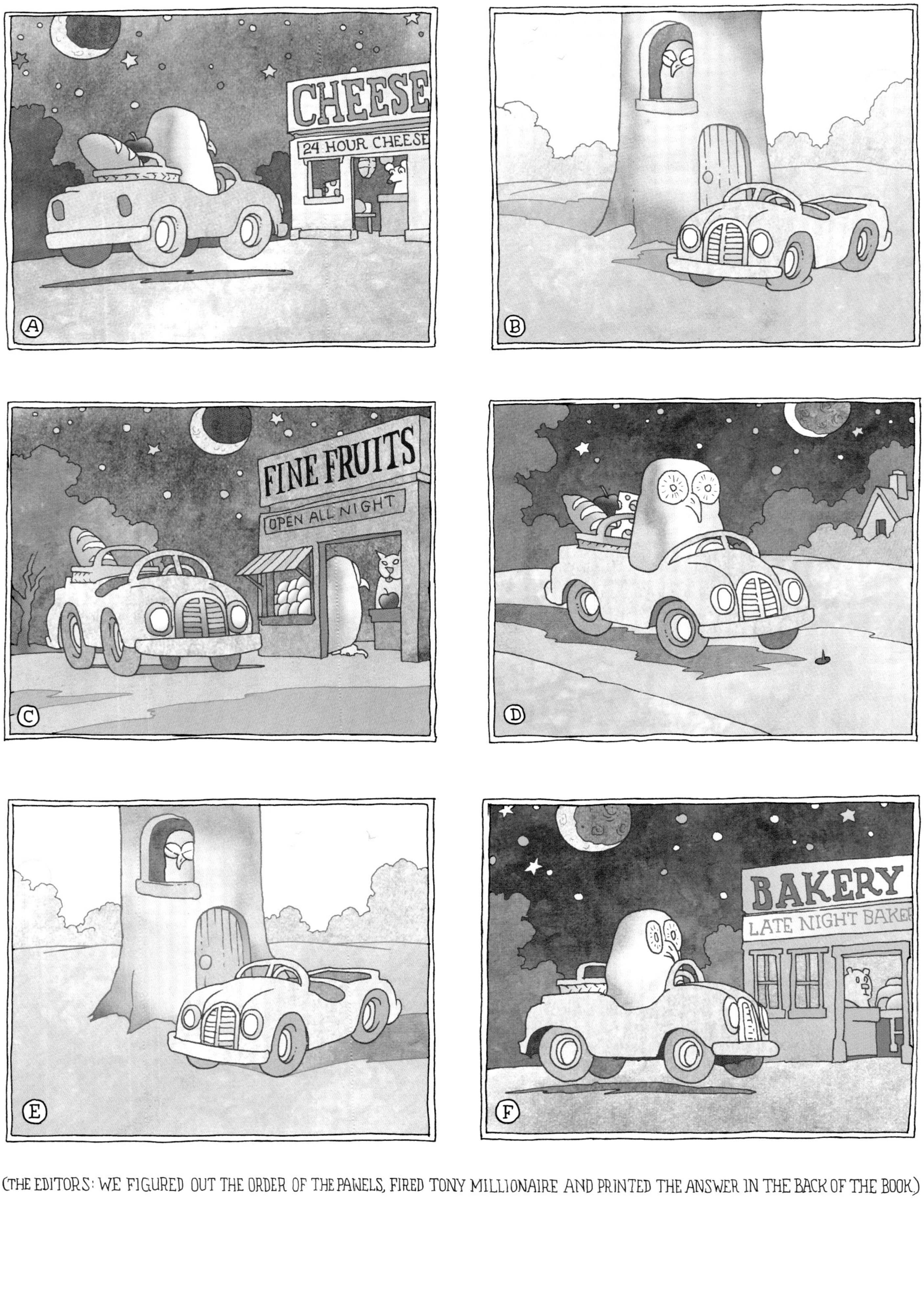
CHEESE
24 HOUR CHEESE
A
B
FINE FRUITS
OPEN ALL NIGHT
C
D
E
BAKERY
LATE NIGHT BAKER
F

(THE EDITORS: WE FIGURED OUT THE ORDER OF THE PANELS, FIRED TONY MILLIONAIRE AND PRINTED THE ANSWER IN THE BACK OF THE BOOK.)

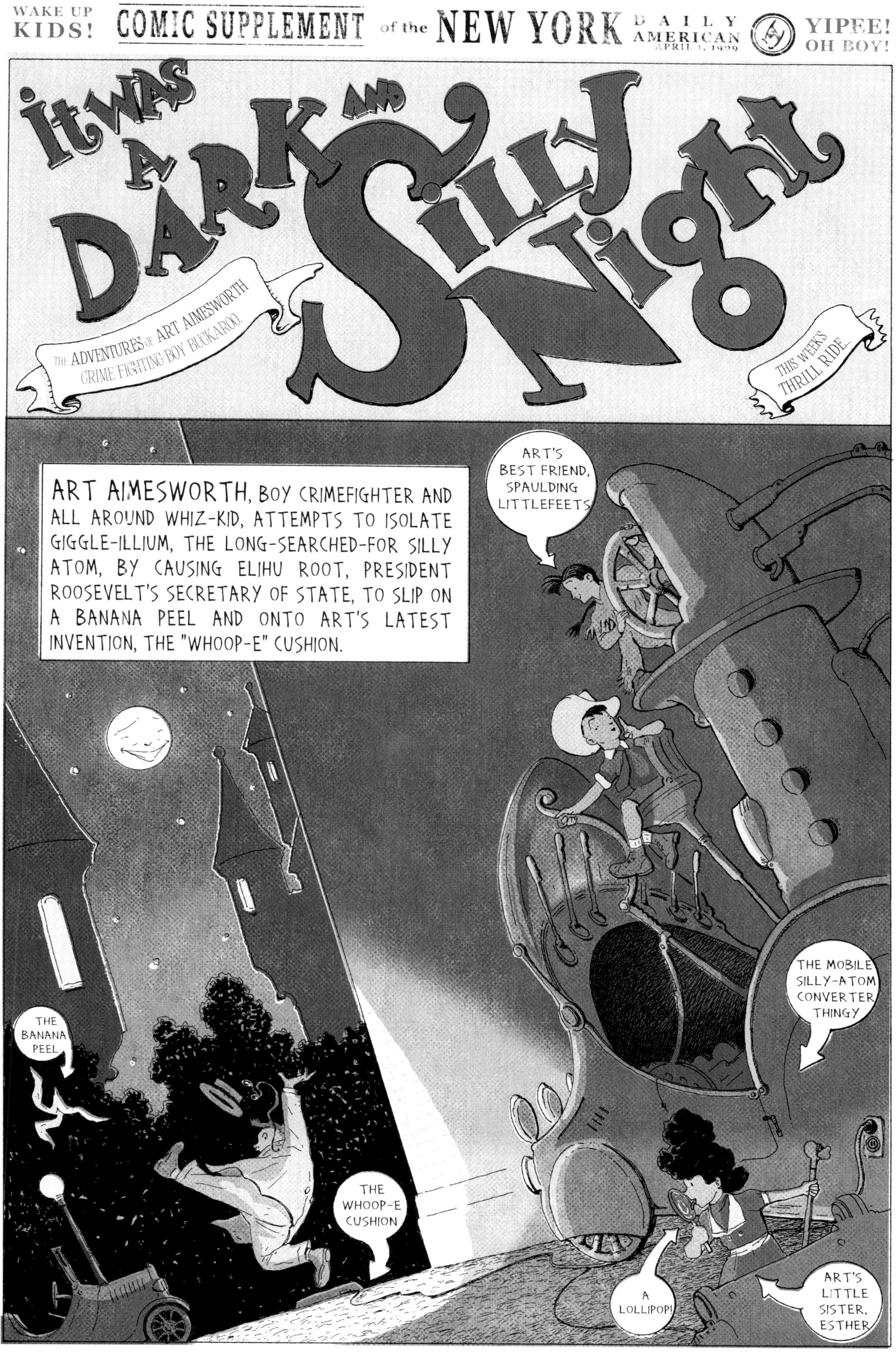
WAKE UP KIDS!
COMIC SUPPLEMENT of the NEW YORK DAILY AMERICAN
APRIL 1, 1909
YIPEE! OH BOY!
It WAS A DARK AND Silly Night
THE ADVENTURES OF ART AIMESWORTH CRIME FIGHTING BOY BUCKAROO.
THIS WEEK'S THRILL RIDE...
ART AIMESWORTH, BOY CRIMEFIGHTER AND ALL AROUND WHIZ-KID, ATTEMPTS TO ISOLATE GIGGLE-ILLIUM, THE LONG-SEARCHED-FOR SILLY ATOM, BY CAUSING ELIHU ROOT, PRESIDENT ROOSEVELT'S SECRETARY OF STATE, TO SLIP ON A BANANA PEEL AND ONTO ART'S LATEST INVENTION, THE "WHOOP-E" CUSHION.
ART'S BEST FRIEND, SPAULDING LITTLEFEETS
THE MOBILE SILLY-ATOM CONVERTER THINGY
THE BANANA PEEL
THE WHOOP-E CUSHION
A LOLLIPOP!
ART'S LITTLE SISTER, ESTHER

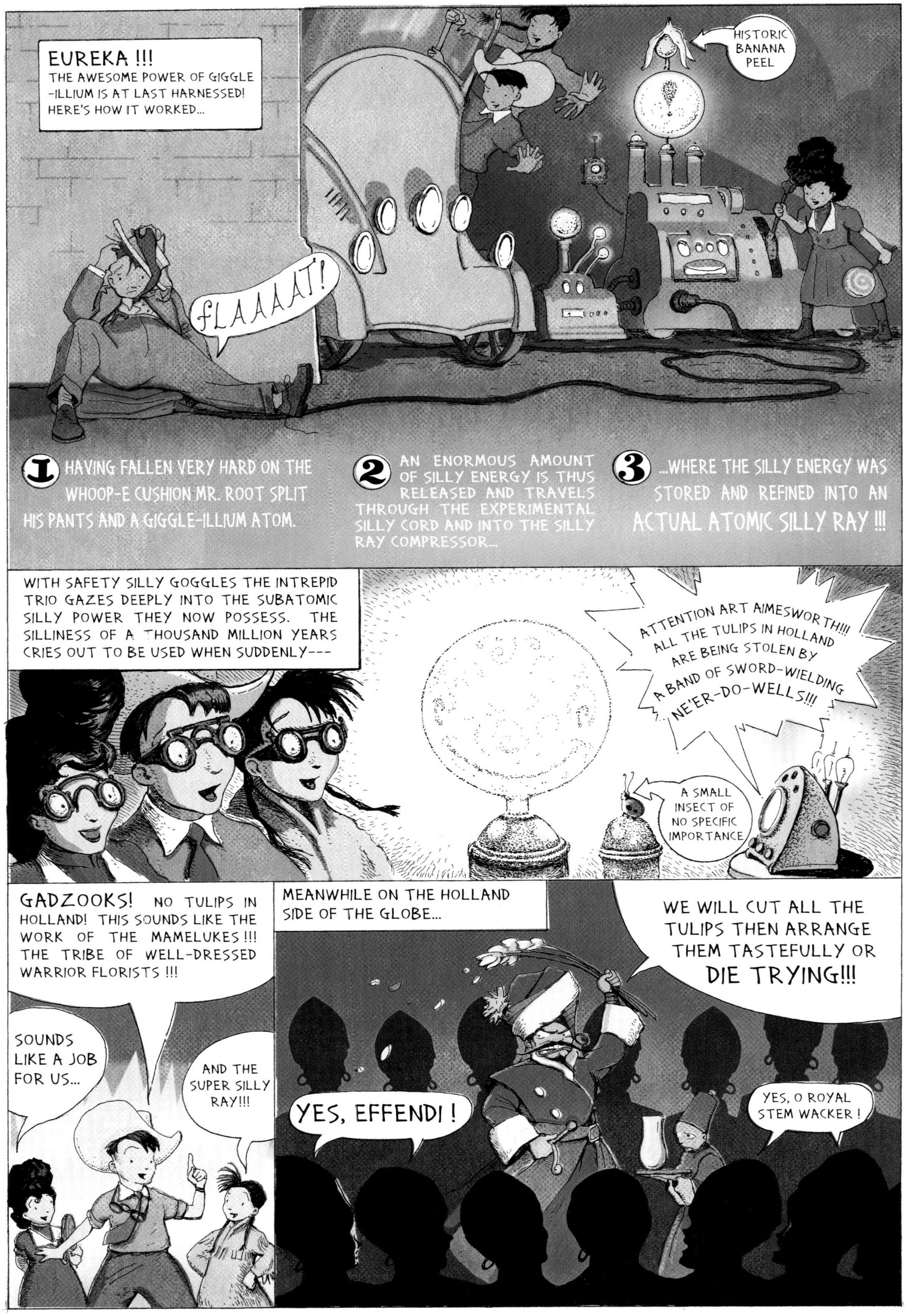
EUREKA !!!
THE AWESOME POWER OF GIGGLE-ILLIUM IS AT LAST HARNESSED! HERE'S HOW IT WORKED...
HISTORIC BANANA PEEL
FLAAAAT!
1 HAVING FALLEN VERY HARD ON THE WHOOP-E CUSHION MR. ROOT SPLIT HIS PANTS AND A GIGGLE-ILLIUM ATOM.
2 AN ENORMOUS AMOUNT OF SILLY ENERGY IS THUS RELEASED AND TRAVELS THROUGH THE EXPERIMENTAL SILLY CORD AND INTO THE SILLY RAY COMPRESSOR...
3 ...WHERE THE SILLY ENERGY WAS STORED AND REFINED INTO AN ACTUAL ATOMIC SILLY RAY !!!
WITH SAFETY SILLY GOGGLES THE INTREPID TRIO GAZES DEEPLY INTO THE SUBATOMIC SILLY POWER THEY NOW POSSESS. THE SILLINESS OF A THOUSAND MILLION YEARS CRIES OUT TO BE USED WHEN SUDDENLY---
ATTENTION ART AIMESWORTH!!! ALL THE TULIPS IN HOLLAND ARE BEING STOLEN BY A BAND OF SWORD-WIELDING NE'ER-DO-WELLS!!!
A SMALL INSECT OF NO SPECIFIC IMPORTANCE
GADZOOKS! NO TULIPS IN HOLLAND! THIS SOUNDS LIKE THE WORK OF THE MAMELUKES!!! THE TRIBE OF WELL-DRESSED WARRIOR FLORISTS !!!
SOUNDS LIKE A JOB FOR US...
AND THE SUPER SILLY RAY!!!
MEANWHILE ON THE HOLLAND SIDE OF THE GLOBE...
WE WILL CUT ALL THE TULIPS THEN ARRANGE THEM TASTEFULLY OR DIE TRYING!!!
YES, EFFENDI !
YES, O ROYAL STEM WACKER !

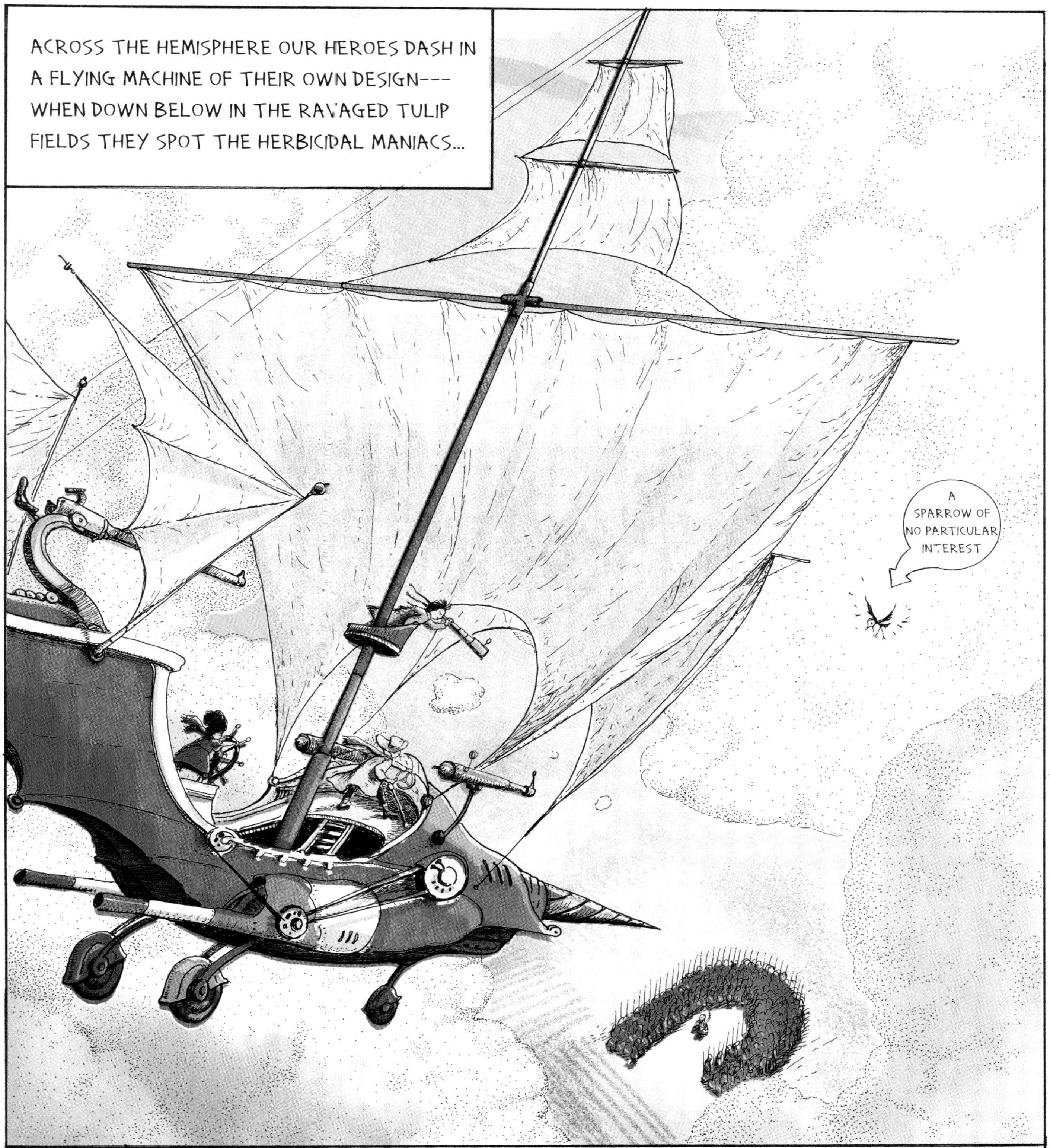
ACROSS THE HEMISPHERE OUR HEROES DASH IN A FLYING MACHINE OF THEIR OWN DESIGN---WHEN DOWN BELOW IN THE RAVAGED TULIP FIELDS THEY SPOT THE HERBICIDAL MANIACS...
A SPARROW OF NO PARTICULAR INTEREST

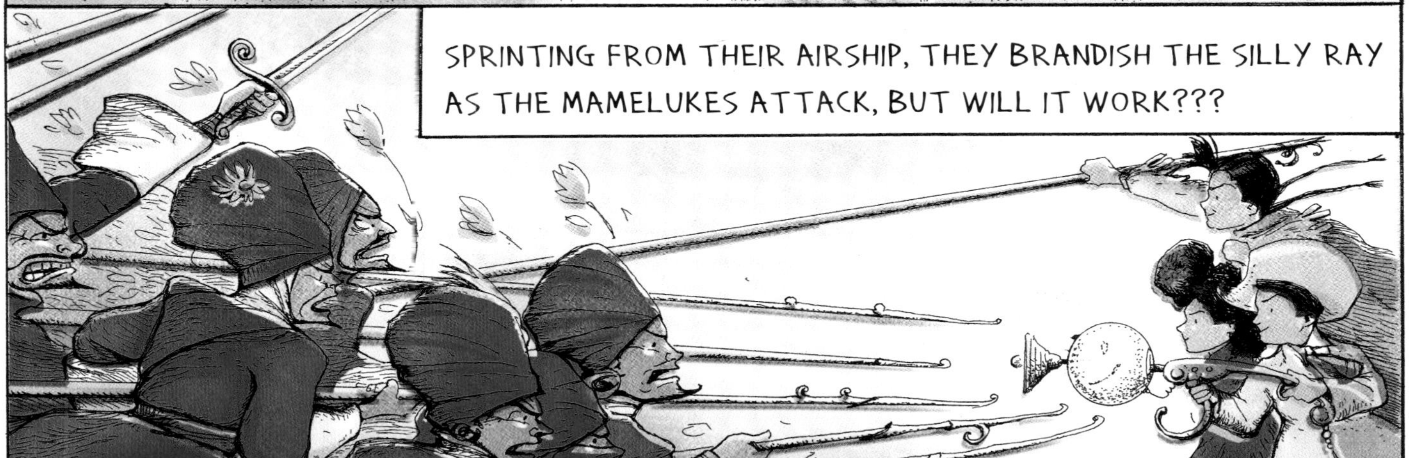
SPRINTING FROM THEIR AIRSHIP, THEY BRANDISH THE SILLY RAY AS THE MAMELUKES ATTACK, BUT WILL IT WORK???

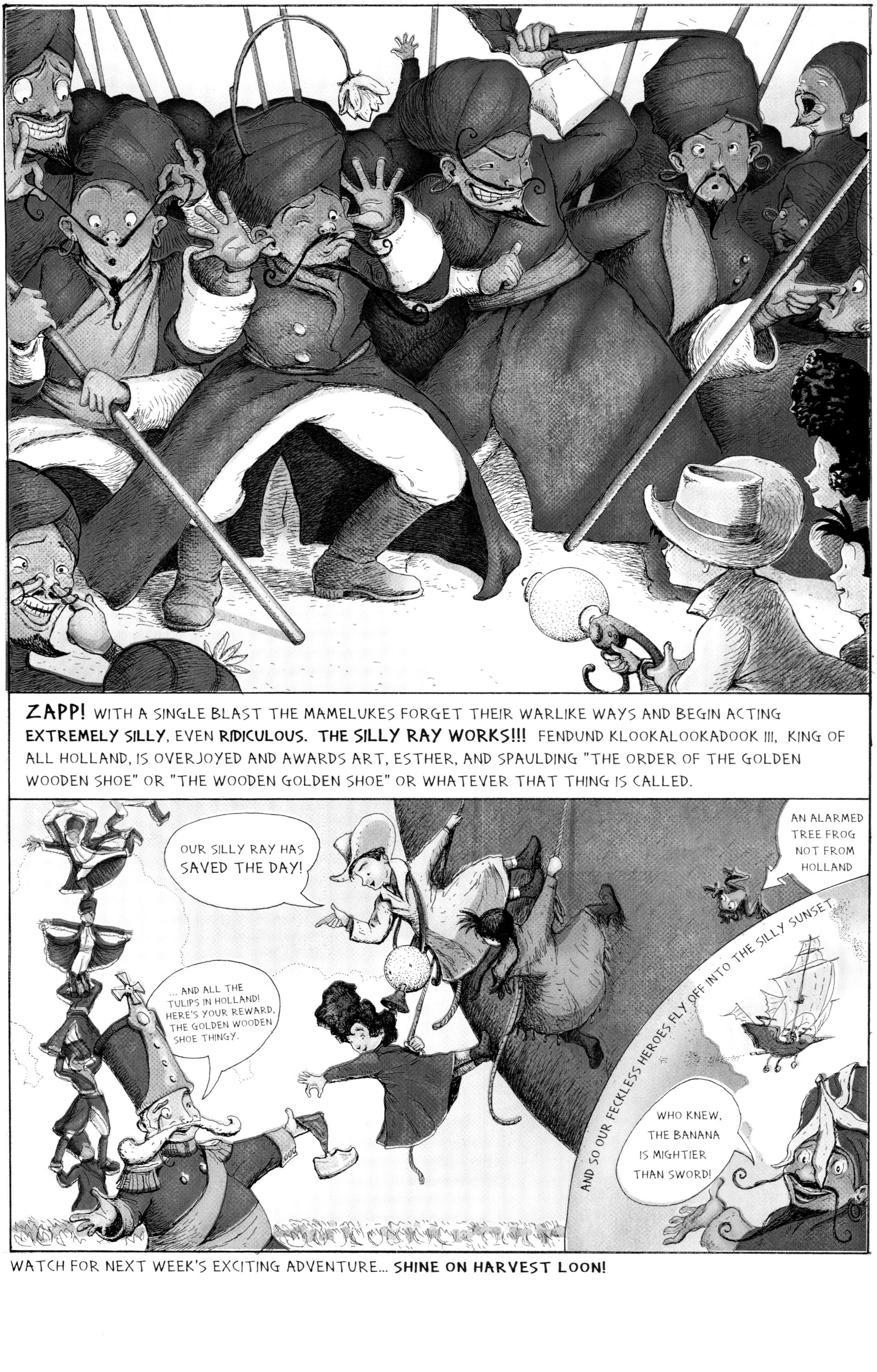
ZAPP! WITH A SINGLE BLAST THE MAMELUKES FORGET THEIR WARLIKE WAYS AND BEGIN ACTING EXTREMELY SILLY, EVEN RIDICULOUS. THE SILLY RAY WORKS!!! FENDUND KLOOKALOOKADOOK III, KING OF ALL HOLLAND, IS OVERJOYED AND AWARDS ART, ESTHER, AND SPAULDING "THE ORDER OF THE GOLDEN WOODEN SHOE" OR "THE WOODEN GOLDEN SHOE" OR WHATEVER THAT THING IS CALLED.
OUR SILLY RAY HAS SAVED THE DAY!
... AND ALL THE TULIPS IN HOLLAND! HERE'S YOUR REWARD, THE GOLDEN WOODEN SHOE THINGY.
AN ALARMED TREE FROG NOT FROM HOLLAND
AND SO OUR FECKLESS HEROES FLY OFF INTO THE SILLY SUNSET.
WHO KNEW, THE BANANA IS MIGHTIER THAN SWORD!

WATCH FOR NEXT WEEK'S EXCITING ADVENTURE... **SHINE ON HARVEST LOON!**

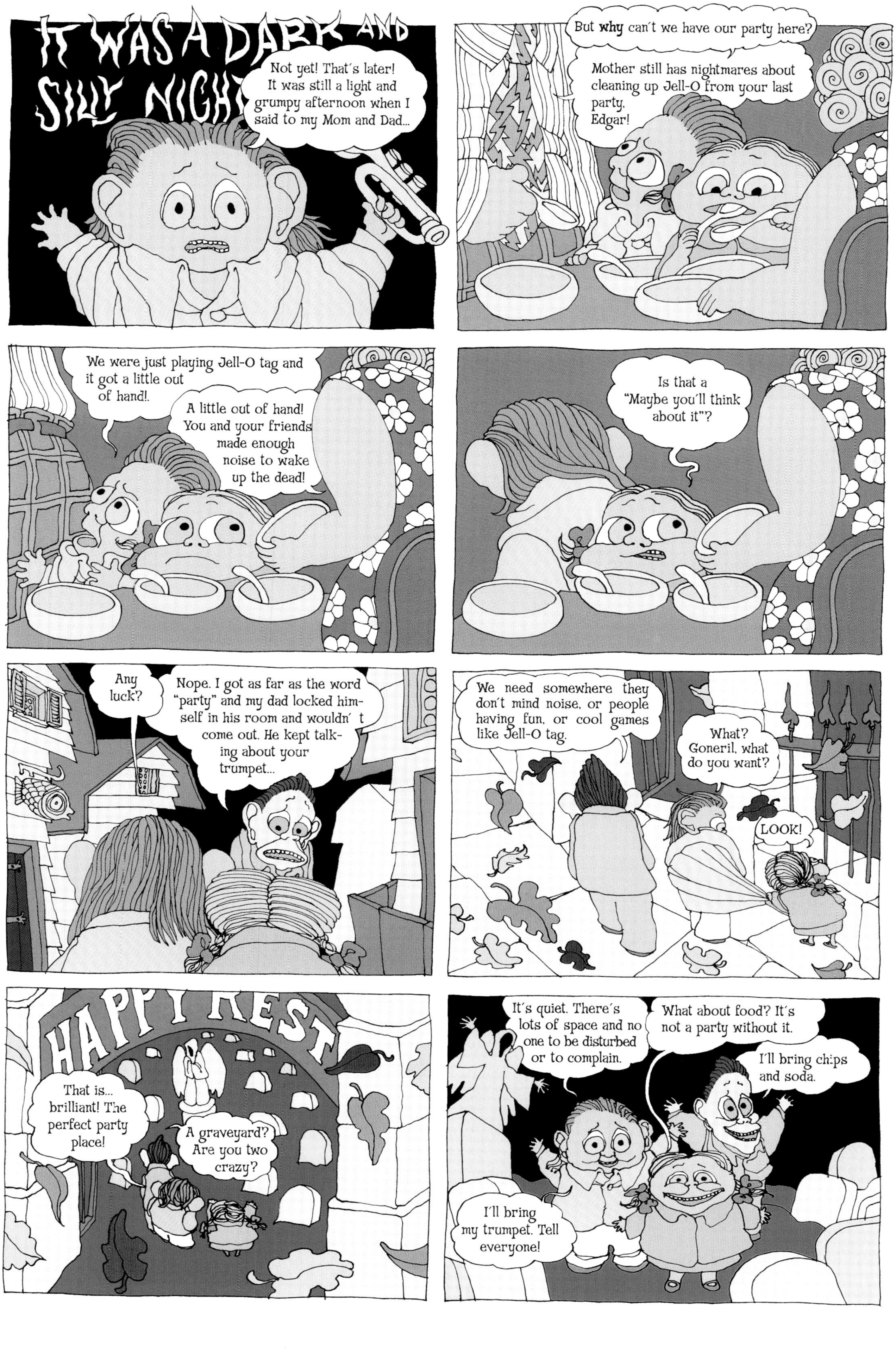
IT WAS A DARK AND
SILLY NIGH
Not yet! That's later! It was still a light and grumpy afternoon when I said to my Mom and Dad...
But **why** can't we have our party here?
Mother still has nightmares about cleaning up Jell-O from your last party, Edgar!
We were just playing Jell-O tag and it got a little out of hand!.
A little out of hand! You and your friends made enough noise to wake up the dead!
Is that a "Maybe you'll think about it"?
Any luck?
Nope. I got as far as the word "party" and my dad locked himself in his room and wouldn' t come out. He kept talking about your trumpet...
We need somewhere they don't mind noise, or people having fun, or cool games like Jell-O tag.
What? Goneril, what do you want?
LOOK!
HAPPY REST
That is... brilliant! The perfect party place!
A graveyard? Are you two crazy?
It's quiet. There's lots of space and no one to be disturbed or to complain.
What about food? It's not a party without it.
I'll bring chips and soda.
I'll bring my trumpet. Tell everyone!

And so...

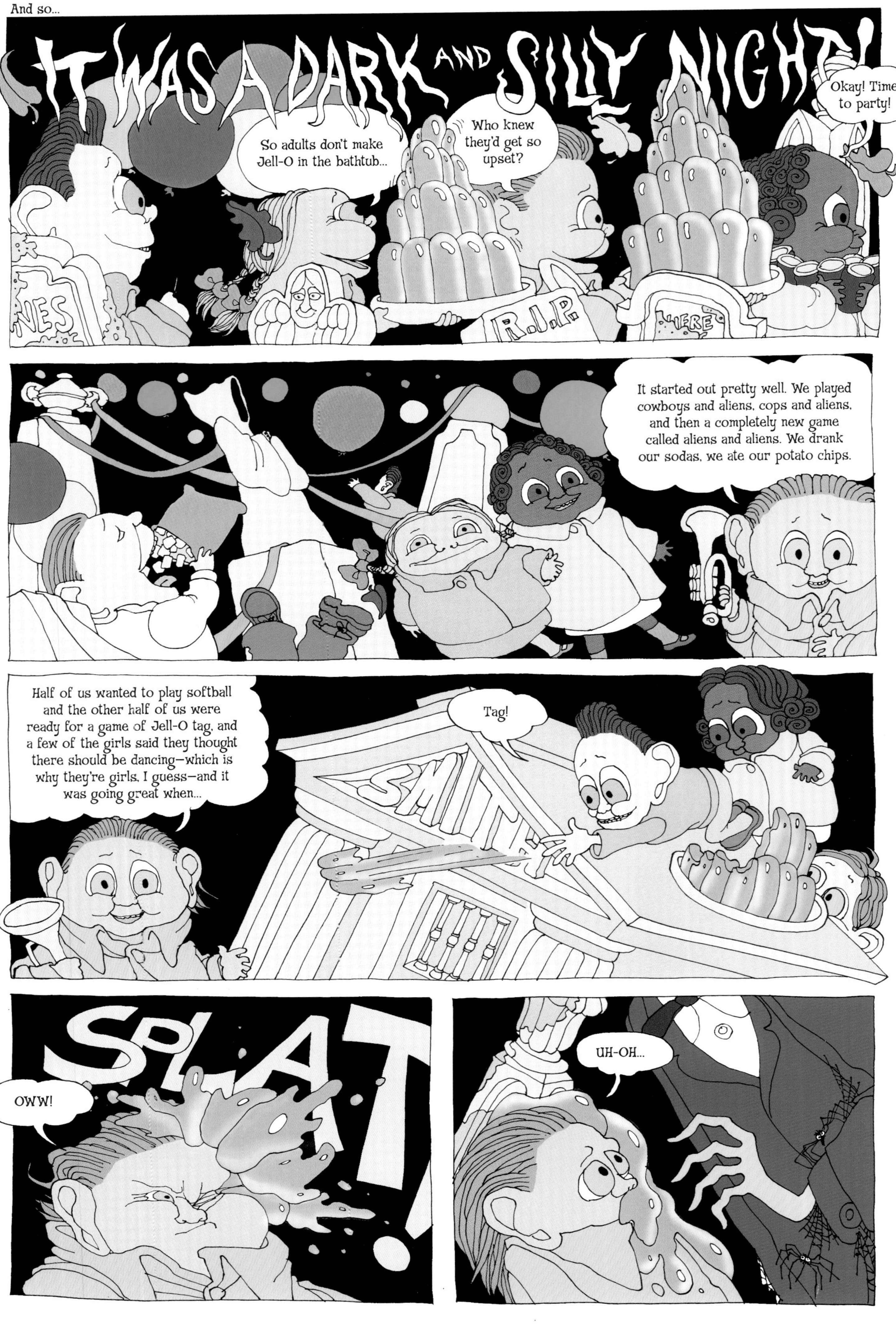
IT WAS A DARK AND SILLY NIGHT!
So adults don't make Jell-O in the bathtub...
Who knew they'd get so upset?
Okay! Time to party!
NES
R.I.P.
HERE
It started out pretty well. We played cowboys and aliens, cops and aliens, and then a completely new game called aliens and aliens. We drank our sodas, we ate our potato chips.
Half of us wanted to play softball and the other half of us were ready for a game of Jell-O tag, and a few of the girls said they thought there should be dancing—which is why they're girls, I guess—and it was going great when...
Tag!
SMIT
SPLAT!
OWW!
UH-OH...

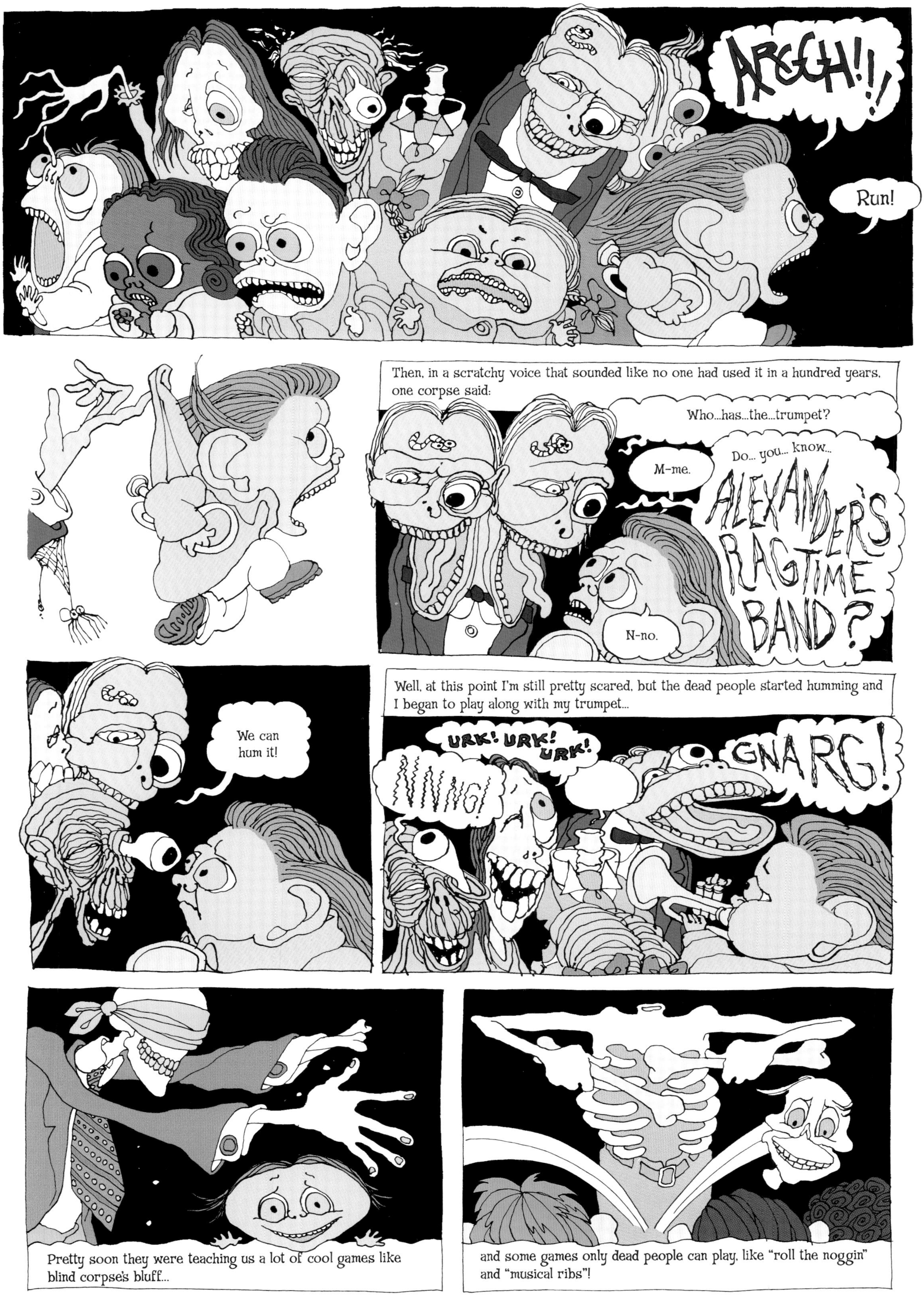
ARGGH!!!
Run!
Then, in a scratchy voice that sounded like no one had used it in a hundred years, one corpse said:
Who...has...the...trumpet?
M-me.
Do... you... know...
ALEXANDER'S RAGTIME BAND?
N-no.
We can hum it!
Well, at this point I'm still pretty scared, but the dead people started humming and I began to play along with my trumpet...
URK! URK! URK!
NNNG!
GNARG!
Pretty soon they were teaching us a lot of cool games like blind corpse's bluff...
and some games only dead people can play, like "roll the noggin" and "musical ribs"!

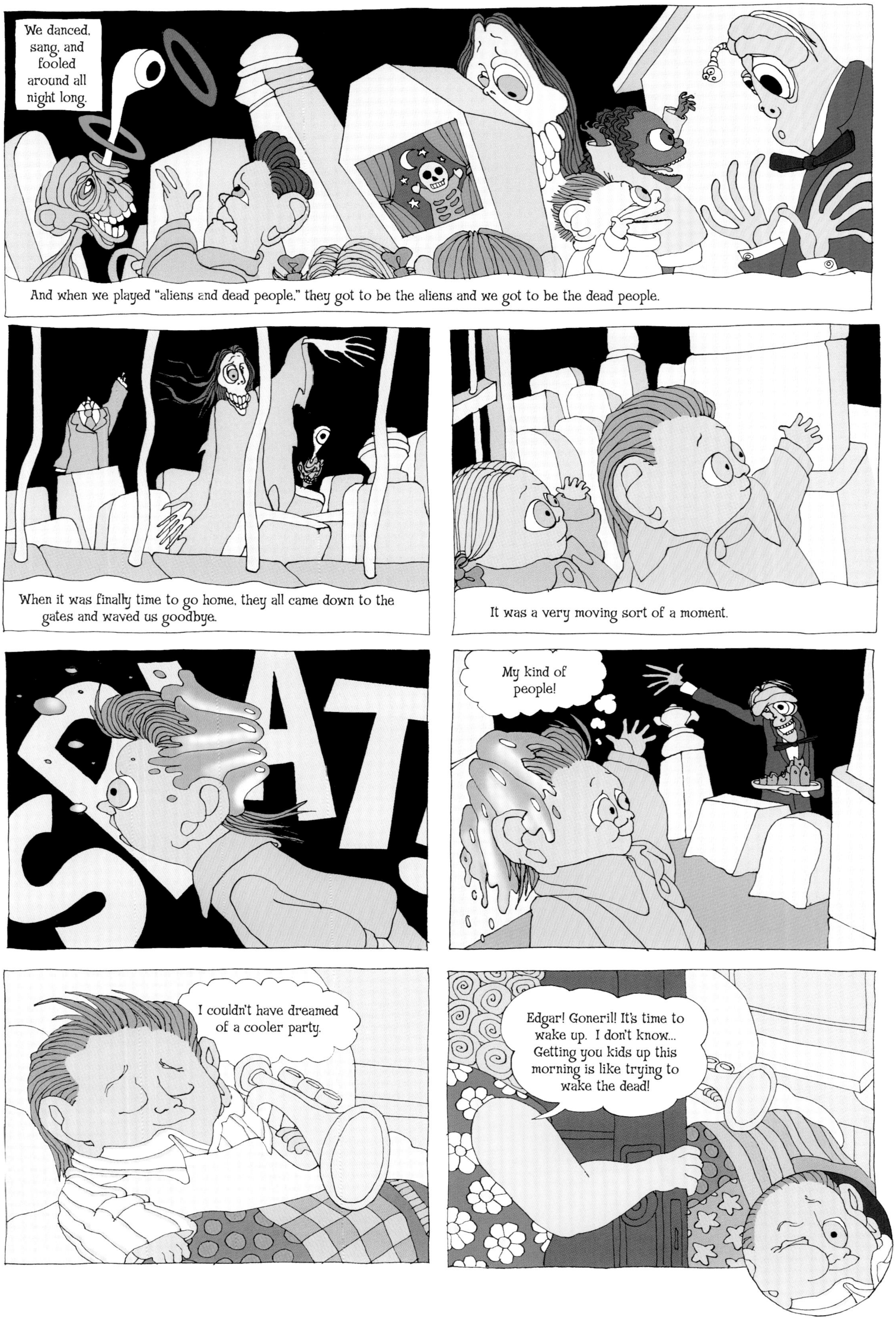
We danced, sang, and fooled around all night long.
And when we played "aliens and dead people," they got to be the aliens and we got to be the dead people.
When it was finally time to go home, they all came down to the gates and waved us goodbye.
It was a very moving sort of a moment.
My kind of people!
I couldn't have dreamed of a cooler party.
Edgar! Goneril! It's time to wake up. I don't know... Getting you kids up this morning is like trying to wake the dead!

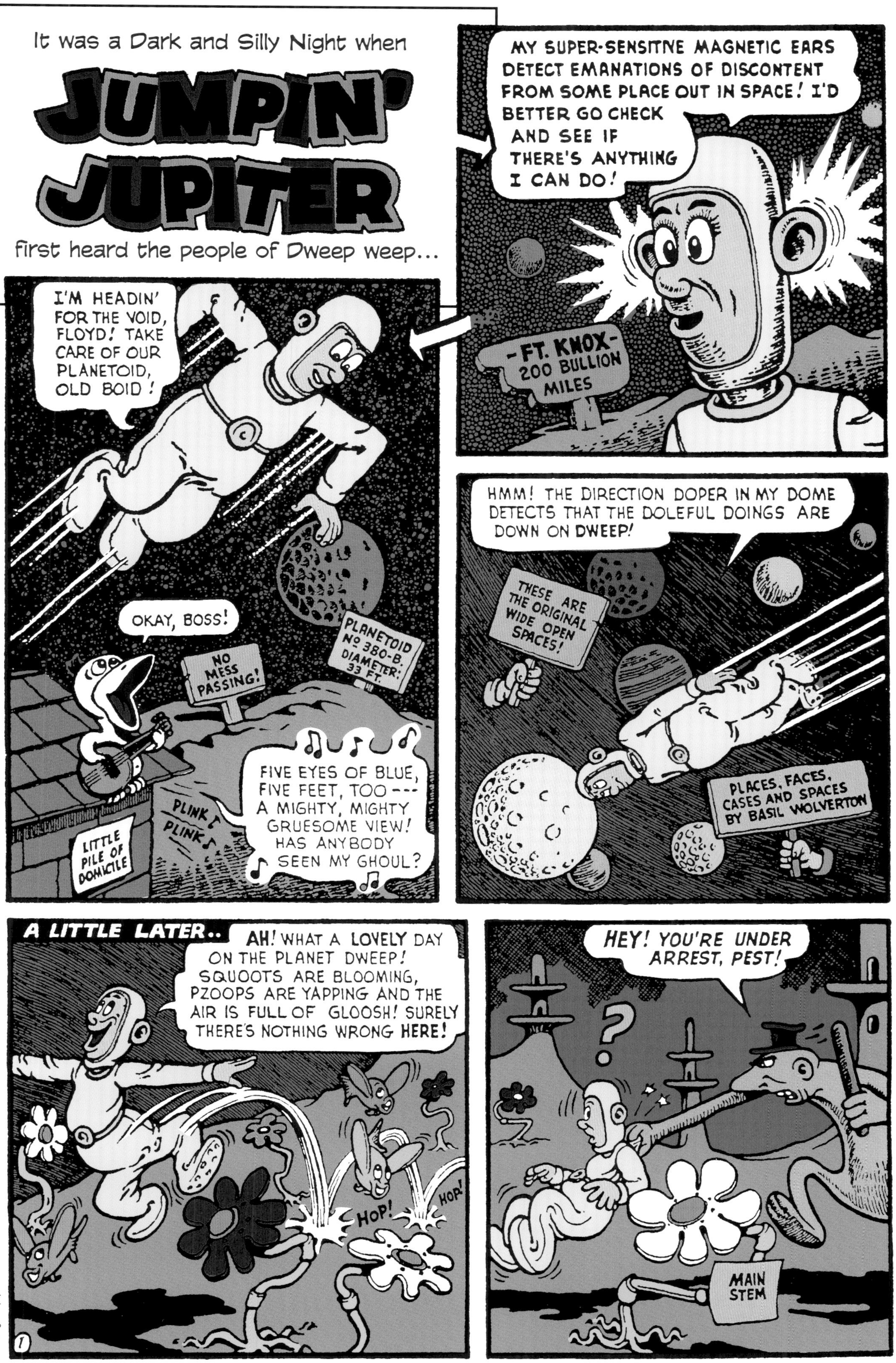
It was a Dark and Silly Night when
JUMPIN' JUPITER
first heard the people of Dweep weep...
MY SUPER-SENSITIVE MAGNETIC EARS DETECT EMANATIONS OF DISCONTENT FROM SOME PLACE OUT IN SPACE! I'D BETTER GO CHECK AND SEE IF THERE'S ANYTHING I CAN DO!
-FT. KNOX- 200 BULLION MILES
I'M HEADIN' FOR THE VOID, FLOYD! TAKE CARE OF OUR PLANETOID, OLD BOID!
OKAY, BOSS!
NO MESS PASSING!
PLANETOID No 380-B. DIAMETER: 33 FT.
FIVE EYES OF BLUE, FIVE FEET, TOO --- A MIGHTY, MIGHTY GRUESOME VIEW! HAS ANYBODY SEEN MY GHOUL?
PLINK PLINK
LITTLE PILE OF DOMICILE
HMM! THE DIRECTION DOPER IN MY DOME DETECTS THAT THE DOLEFUL DOINGS ARE DOWN ON DWEEP!
THESE ARE THE ORIGINAL WIDE OPEN SPACES!
PLACES, FACES, CASES AND SPACES BY BASIL WOLVERTON
A LITTLE LATER..
AH! WHAT A LOVELY DAY ON THE PLANET DWEEP! SQUOOTS ARE BLOOMING, PZOOPS ARE YAPPING AND THE AIR IS FULL OF GLOOSH! SURELY THERE'S NOTHING WRONG HERE!
HOP! HOP!
1
HEY! YOU'RE UNDER ARREST, PEST!
?
MAIN STEM

Originally published in 1952 in *Weird Tales of the Future.*

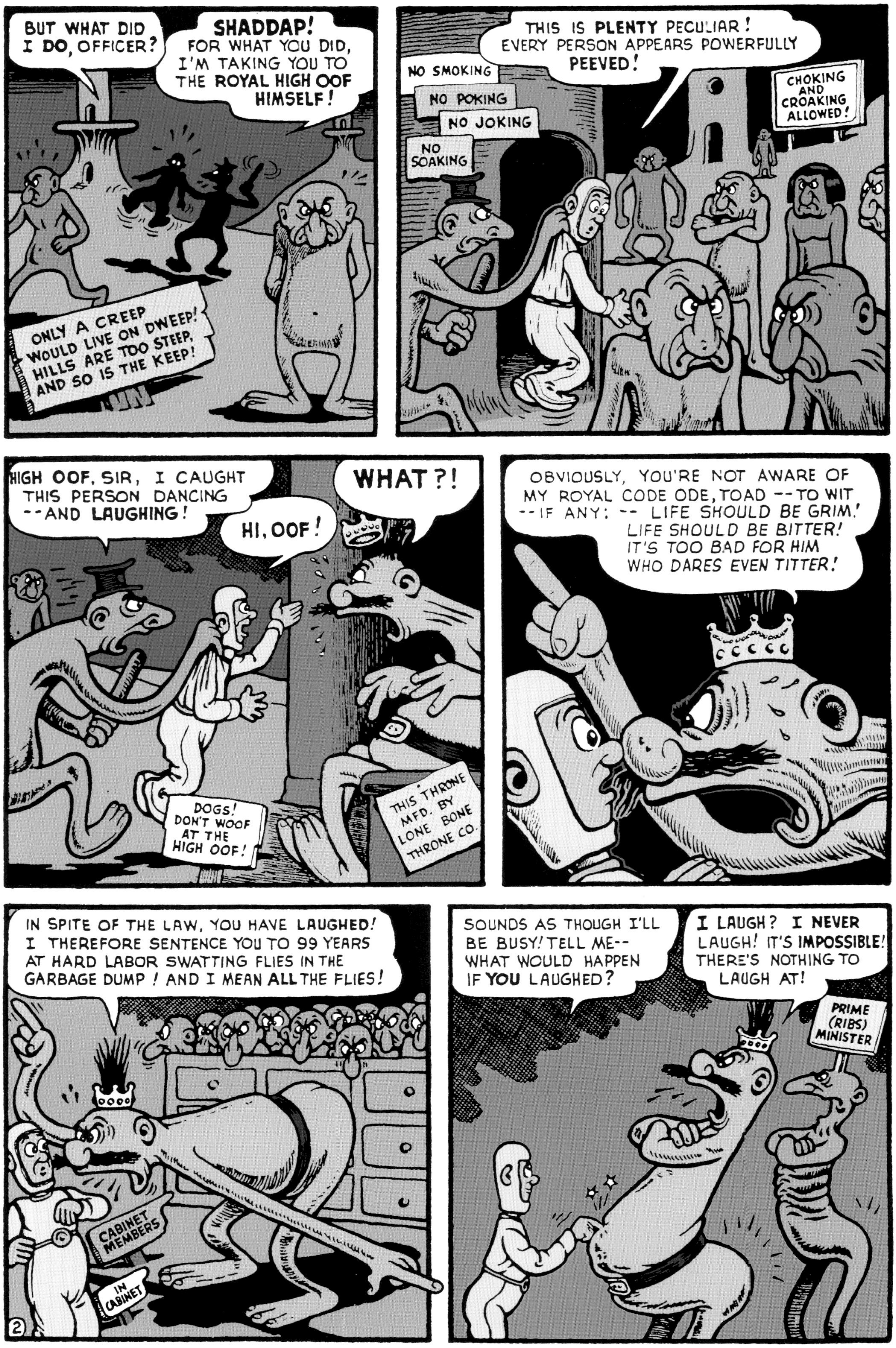

BUT WHAT DID I DO, OFFICER?
SHADDAP! FOR WHAT YOU DID, I'M TAKING YOU TO THE ROYAL HIGH OOF HIMSELF!
ONLY A CREEP WOULD LIVE ON DWEEP! HILLS ARE TOO STEEP, AND SO IS THE KEEP!
THIS IS PLENTY PECULIAR! EVERY PERSON APPEARS POWERFULLY PEEVED!
NO SMOKING
NO POKING
NO JOKING
NO SOAKING
CHOKING AND CROAKING ALLOWED!
HIGH OOF, SIR, I CAUGHT THIS PERSON DANCING --AND LAUGHING!
HI, OOF!
WHAT?!
DOGS! DON'T WOOF AT THE HIGH OOF!
THIS THRONE MFD. BY LONE BONE THRONE CO.
OBVIOUSLY, YOU'RE NOT AWARE OF MY ROYAL CODE ODE, TOAD -- TO WIT -- IF ANY: -- LIFE SHOULD BE GRIM! LIFE SHOULD BE BITTER! IT'S TOO BAD FOR HIM WHO DARES EVEN TITTER!
IN SPITE OF THE LAW, YOU HAVE LAUGHED! I THEREFORE SENTENCE YOU TO 99 YEARS AT HARD LABOR SWATTING FLIES IN THE GARBAGE DUMP! AND I MEAN ALL THE FLIES!
CABINET MEMBERS
IN CABINET
SOUNDS AS THOUGH I'LL BE BUSY! TELL ME-- WHAT WOULD HAPPEN IF YOU LAUGHED?
I LAUGH? I NEVER LAUGH! IT'S IMPOSSIBLE! THERE'S NOTHING TO LAUGH AT!
PRIME (RIBS) MINISTER

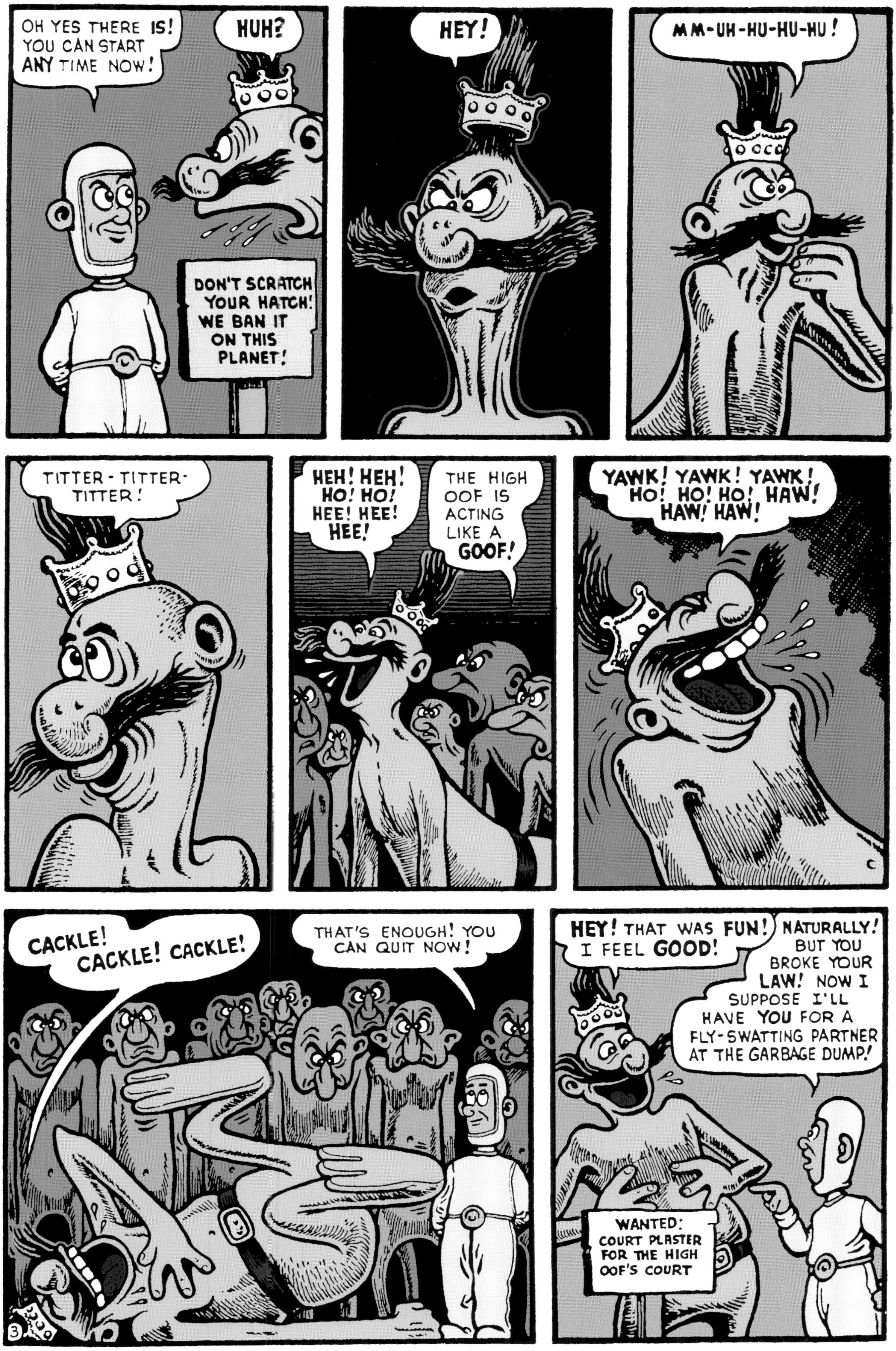
OH YES THERE IS! YOU CAN START ANY TIME NOW!
HUH?
DON'T SCRATCH YOUR HATCH! WE BAN IT ON THIS PLANET!
HEY!
MM-UH-HU-HU-HU!
TITTER-TITTER-TITTER!
HEH! HEH! HO! HO! HEE! HEE! HEE!
THE HIGH OOF IS ACTING LIKE A GOOF!
YAWK! YAWK! YAWK! HO! HO! HO! HAW! HAW! HAW!
CACKLE! CACKLE! CACKLE!
THAT'S ENOUGH! YOU CAN QUIT NOW!
HEY! THAT WAS FUN! I FEEL GOOD!
NATURALLY! BUT YOU BROKE YOUR LAW! NOW I SUPPOSE I'LL HAVE YOU FOR A FLY-SWATTING PARTNER AT THE GARBAGE DUMP!
WANTED: COURT PLASTER FOR THE HIGH OOF'S COURT

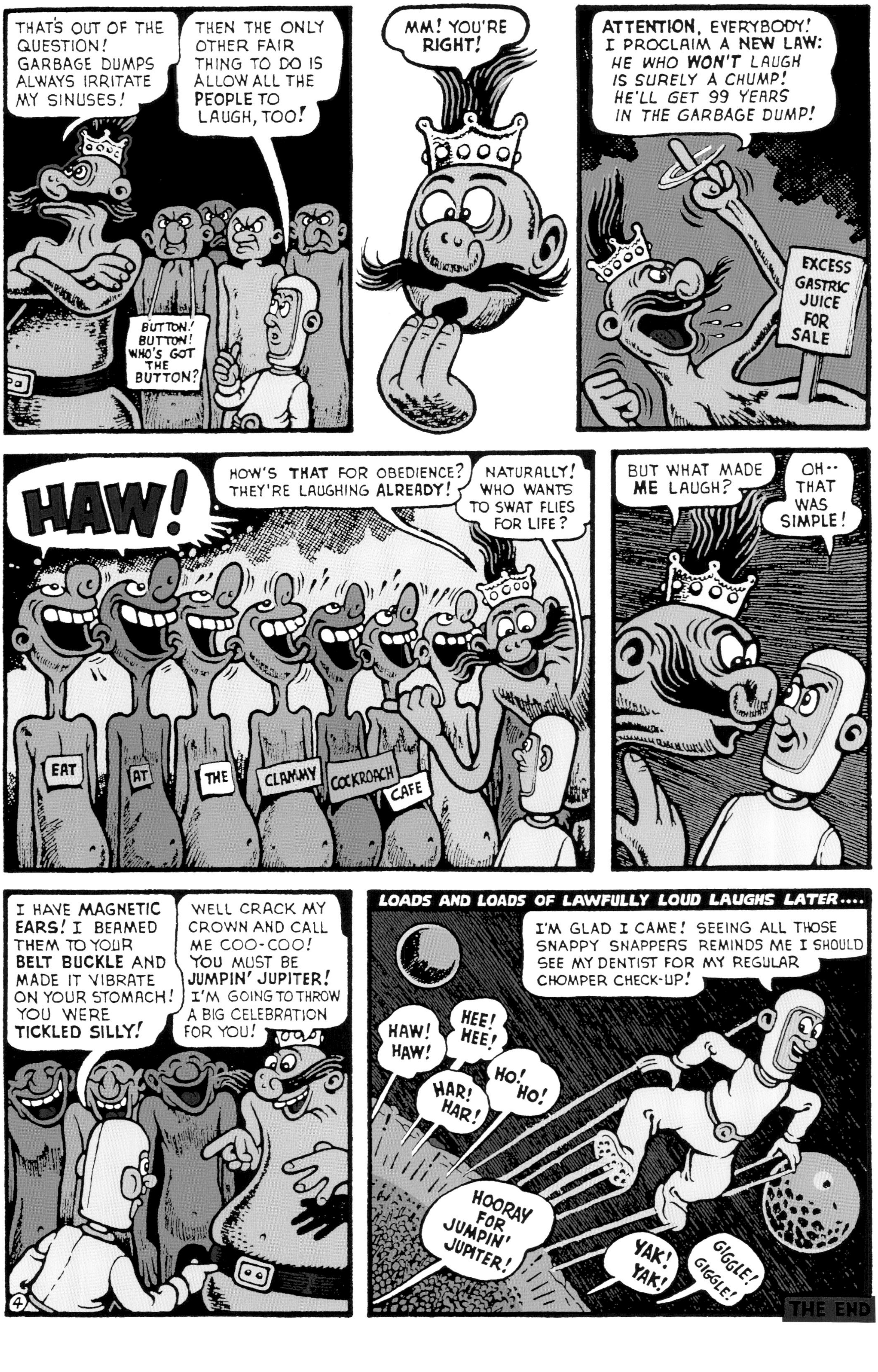
THAT'S OUT OF THE QUESTION! GARBAGE DUMPS ALWAYS IRRITATE MY SINUSES!
THEN THE ONLY OTHER FAIR THING TO DO IS ALLOW ALL THE PEOPLE TO LAUGH, TOO!
BUTTON! BUTTON! WHO'S GOT THE BUTTON?
MM! YOU'RE RIGHT!
ATTENTION, EVERYBODY! I PROCLAIM A NEW LAW: HE WHO WON'T LAUGH IS SURELY A CHUMP! HE'LL GET 99 YEARS IN THE GARBAGE DUMP!
EXCESS GASTRIC JUICE FOR SALE
HAW!
HOW'S THAT FOR OBEDIENCE? THEY'RE LAUGHING ALREADY!
NATURALLY! WHO WANTS TO SWAT FLIES FOR LIFE?
EAT AT THE CLAMMY COCKROACH CAFE
BUT WHAT MADE ME LAUGH?
OH.. THAT WAS SIMPLE!
I HAVE MAGNETIC EARS! I BEAMED THEM TO YOUR BELT BUCKLE AND MADE IT VIBRATE ON YOUR STOMACH! YOU WERE TICKLED SILLY!
WELL CRACK MY CROWN AND CALL ME COO-COO! YOU MUST BE JUMPIN' JUPITER! I'M GOING TO THROW A BIG CELEBRATION FOR YOU!
4
LOADS AND LOADS OF LAWFULLY LOUD LAUGHS LATER....
I'M GLAD I CAME! SEEING ALL THOSE SNAPPY SNAPPERS REMINDS ME I SHOULD SEE MY DENTIST FOR MY REGULAR CHOMPER CHECK-UP!
HAW! HAW!
HEE! HEE!
HO! HO!
HAR! HAR!
HOORAY FOR JUMPIN' JUPITER!
YAK! YAK!
GIGGLE! GIGGLE!
THE END

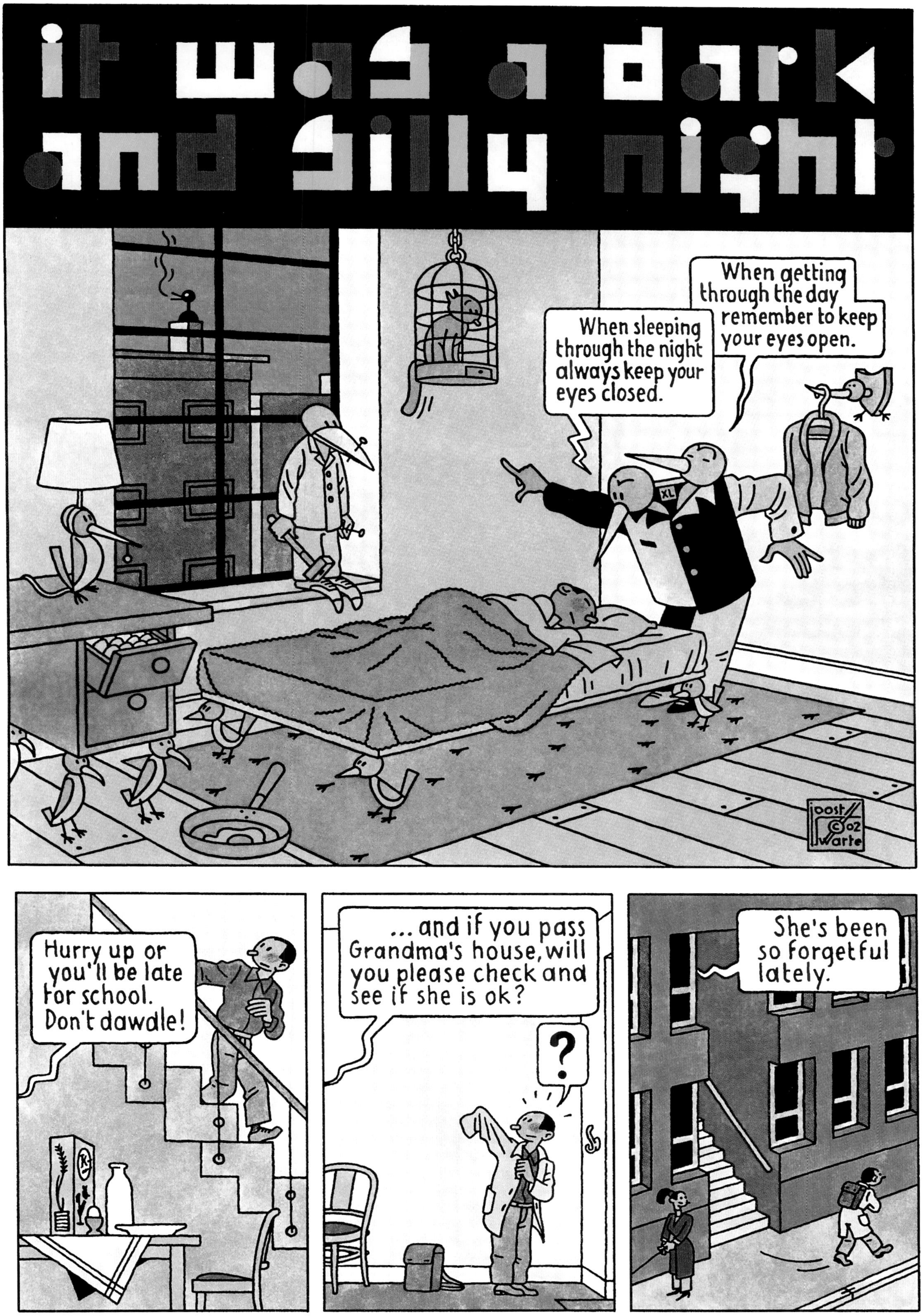
it was a dark and silly night
When sleeping through the night always keep your eyes closed.
When getting through the day remember to keep your eyes open.
XL
joost ©02 swarte
Hurry up or you'll be late for school. Don't dawdle!
... and if you pass Grandma's house, will you please check and see if she is ok?
?
She's been so forgetful lately.

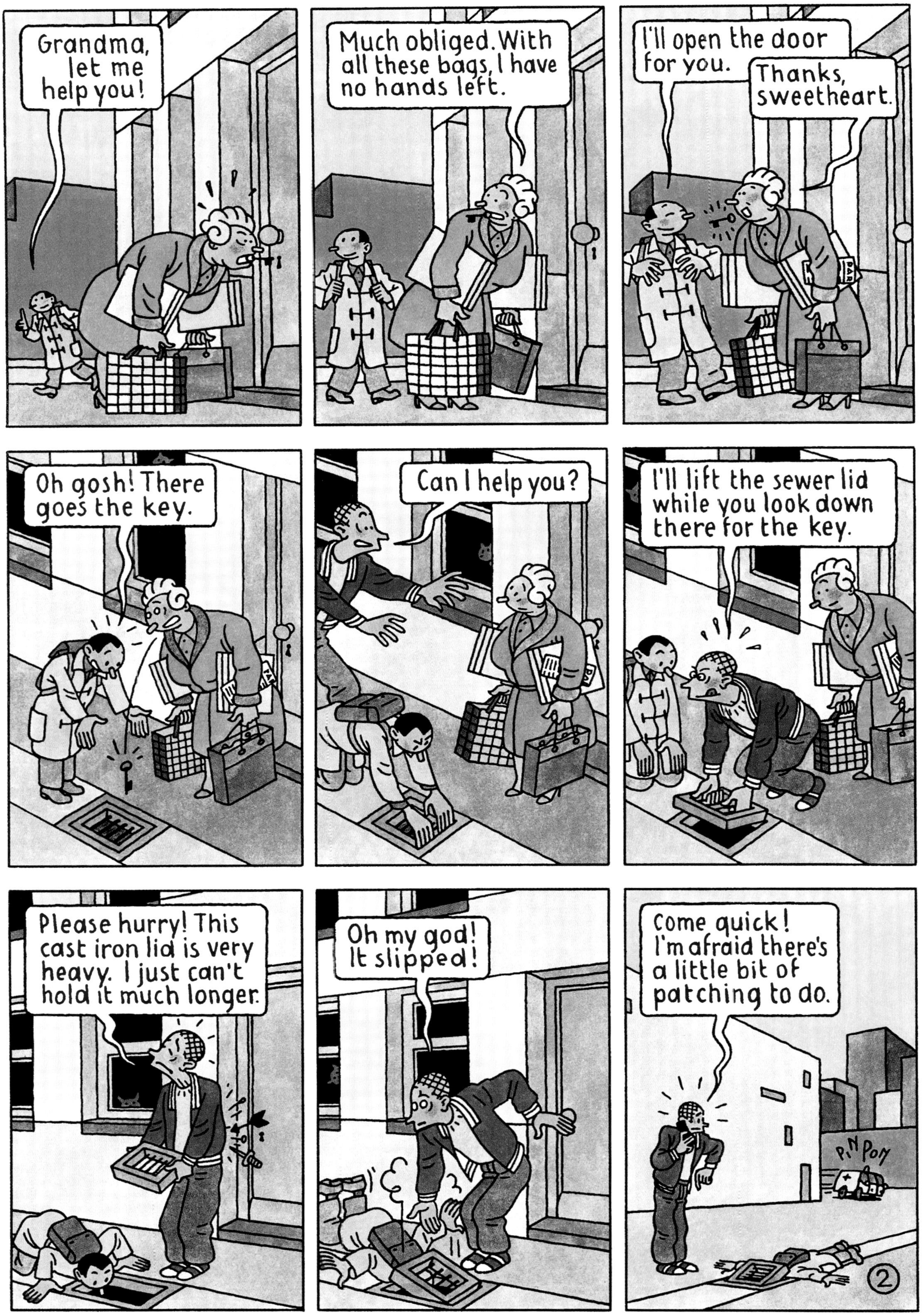
Grandma, let me help you!
Much obliged. With all these bags, I have no hands left.
I'll open the door for you.
Thanks, sweetheart.
Oh gosh! There goes the key.
Can I help you?
I'll lift the sewer lid while you look down there for the key.
Please hurry! This cast iron lid is very heavy. I just can't hold it much longer.
Oh my god! It slipped!
Come quick! I'm afraid there's a little bit of patching to do.
PiN PoN
2

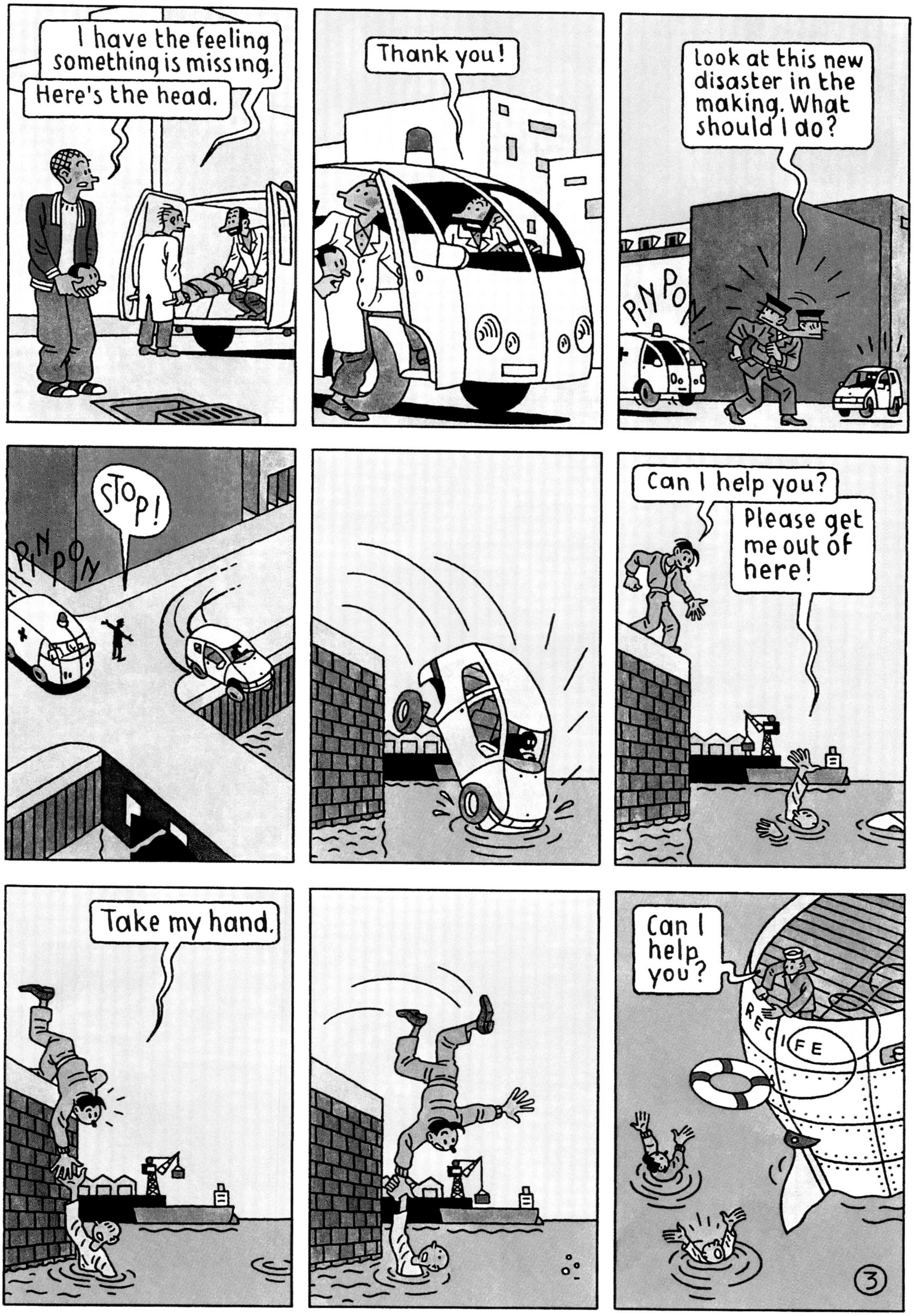
I have the feeling something is missing.
Here's the head.
Thank you!
Look at this new disaster in the making. What should I do?
PIN PON
PIN PON
STOP!
Can I help you?
Please get me out of here!
Take my hand.
Can I help you?
RECIFE
3

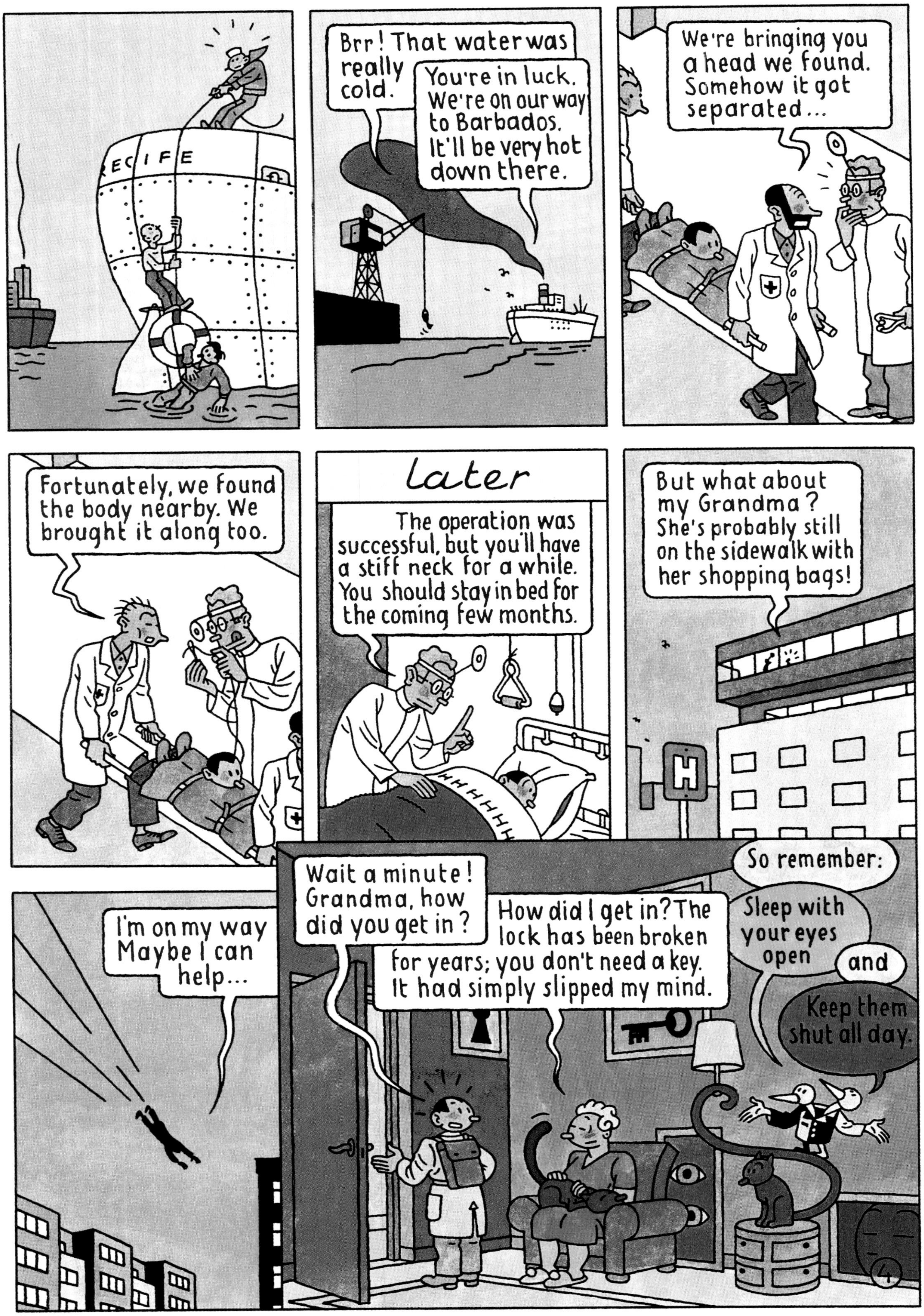

Brr! That water was really cold.
You're in luck. We're on our way to Barbados. It'll be very hot down there.
We're bringing you a head we found. Somehow it got separated...
Fortunately, we found the body nearby. We brought it along too.
later
The operation was successful, but you'll have a stiff neck for a while. You should stay in bed for the coming few months.
But what about my Grandma? She's probably still on the sidewalk with her shopping bags!
I'm on my way Maybe I can help...
Wait a minute! Grandma, how did you get in?
How did I get in? The lock has been broken for years; you don't need a key. It had simply slipped my mind.
So remember:
Sleep with your eyes open
and
Keep them shut all day.

carlos nine

It Was a Dark and Silly Night

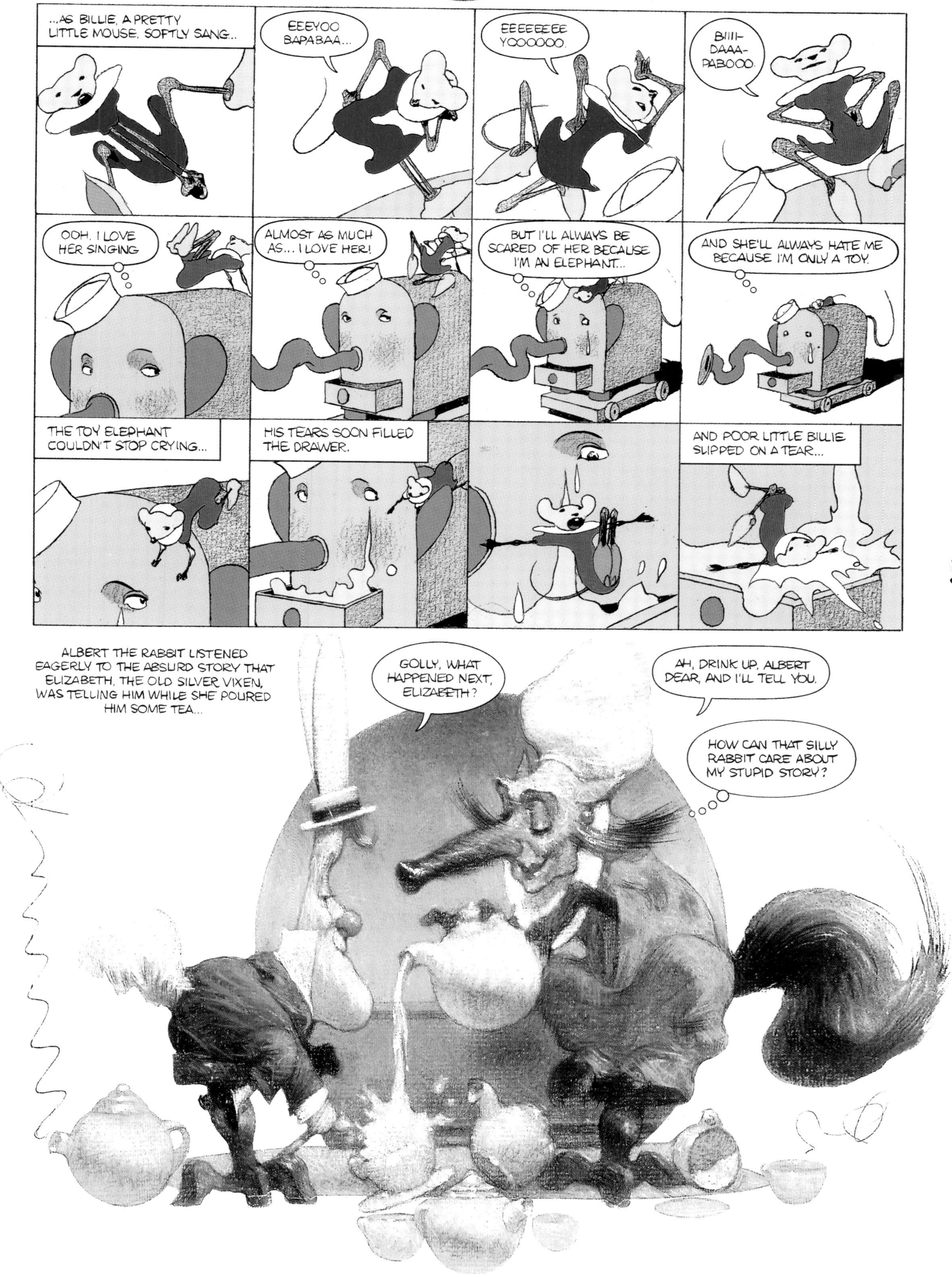

...AS BILLIE, A PRETTY LITTLE MOUSE, SOFTLY SANG...
EEEYOO BAPABAA...
EEEEEEEE YOOOOOO.
BIIII-DAAA-PABOOO.
OOH, I LOVE HER SINGING
ALMOST AS MUCH AS... I LOVE HER!
BUT I'LL ALWAYS BE SCARED OF HER BECAUSE I'M AN ELEPHANT...
AND SHE'LL ALWAYS HATE ME BECAUSE I'M ONLY A TOY.
THE TOY ELEPHANT COULDN'T STOP CRYING...
HIS TEARS SOON FILLED THE DRAWER.
AND POOR LITTLE BILLIE SLIPPED ON A TEAR...
ALBERT THE RABBIT LISTENED EAGERLY TO THE ABSURD STORY THAT ELIZABETH, THE OLD SILVER VIXEN, WAS TELLING HIM WHILE SHE POURED HIM SOME TEA...
GOLLY, WHAT HAPPENED NEXT, ELIZABETH?
AH, DRINK UP, ALBERT DEAR, AND I'LL TELL YOU.
HOW CAN THAT SILLY RABBIT CARE ABOUT MY STUPID STORY?

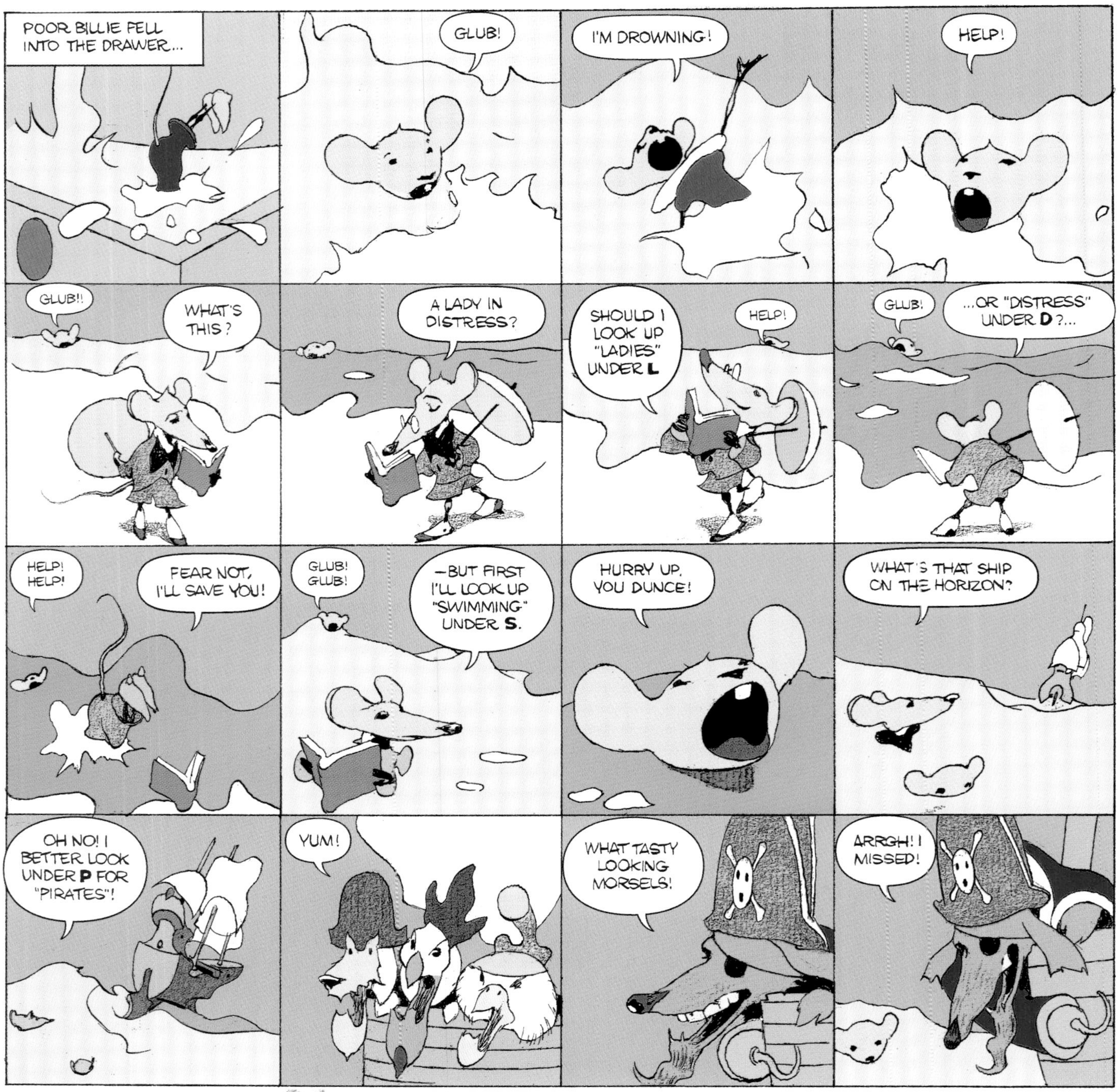
POOR BILLIE FELL INTO THE DRAWER...
GLUB!
I'M DROWNING!
HELP!
GLUB!!
WHAT'S THIS?
A LADY IN DISTRESS?
SHOULD I LOOK UP "LADIES" UNDER **L**
HELP!
GLUB!
...OR "DISTRESS" UNDER **D**?...
HELP! HELP!
FEAR NOT, I'LL SAVE YOU!
GLUB! GLUB!
—BUT FIRST I'LL LOOK UP "SWIMMING" UNDER **S**.
HURRY UP, YOU DUNCE!
WHAT'S THAT SHIP ON THE HORIZON?
OH NO! I BETTER LOOK UNDER **P** FOR "PIRATES"!
YUM!
WHAT TASTY LOOKING MORSELS!
ARRGH! I MISSED!

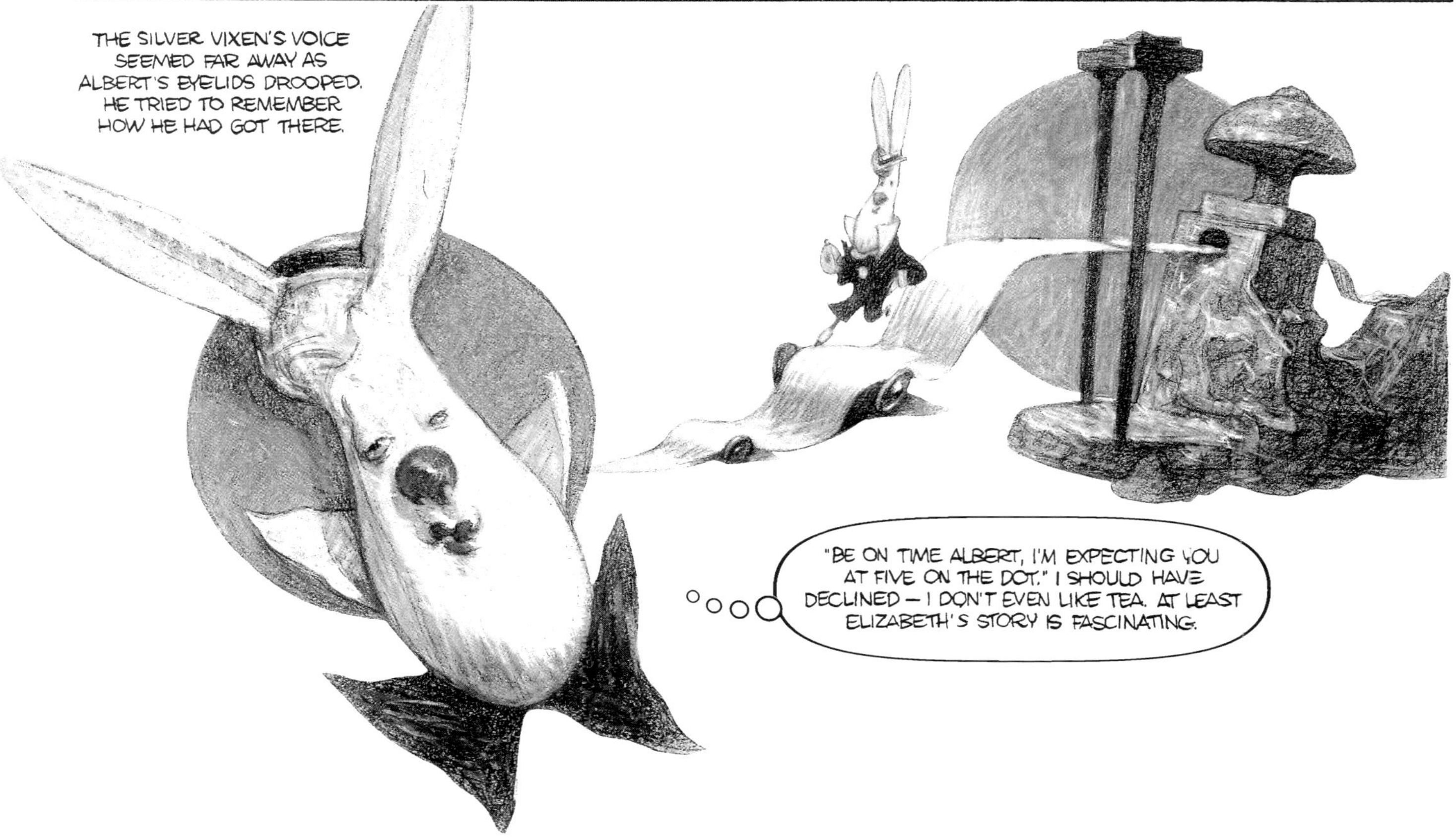
THE SILVER VIXEN'S VOICE SEEMED FAR AWAY AS ALBERT'S EYELIDS DROOPED. HE TRIED TO REMEMBER HOW HE HAD GOT THERE.
"BE ON TIME ALBERT, I'M EXPECTING YOU AT FIVE ON THE DOT." I SHOULD HAVE DECLINED – I DON'T EVEN LIKE TEA. AT LEAST ELIZABETH'S STORY IS FASCINATING.

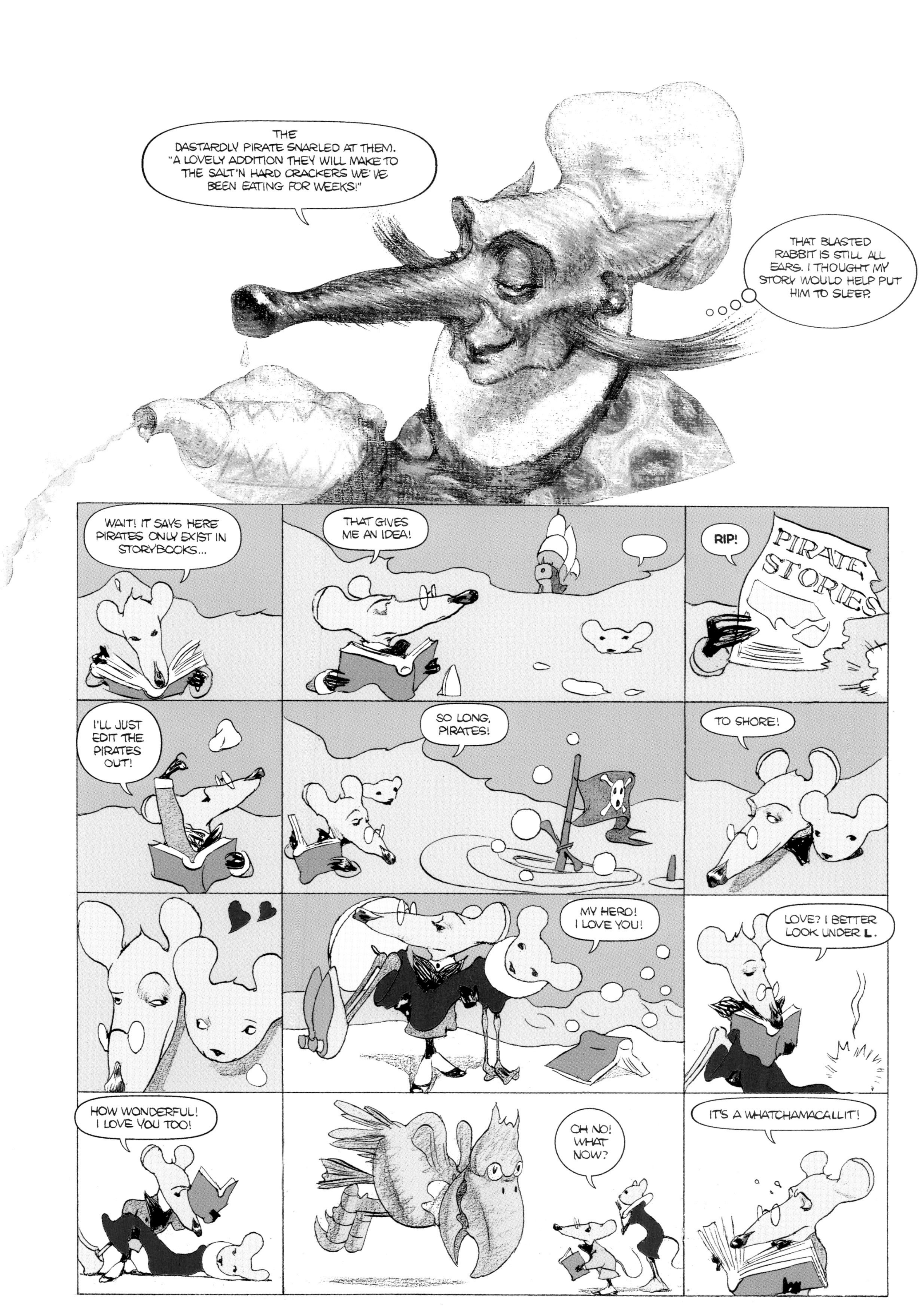

THE DASTARDLY PIRATE SNARLED AT THEM. "A LOVELY ADDITION THEY WILL MAKE TO THE SALT'N HARD CRACKERS WE'VE BEEN EATING FOR WEEKS!"
THAT BLASTED RABBIT IS STILL ALL EARS. I THOUGHT MY STORY WOULD HELP PUT HIM TO SLEEP.
WAIT! IT SAYS HERE PIRATES ONLY EXIST IN STORYBOOKS...
THAT GIVES ME AN IDEA!
RIP!
PIRATE STORIES
I'LL JUST EDIT THE PIRATES OUT!
SO LONG, PIRATES!
TO SHORE!
MY HERO! I LOVE YOU!
LOVE? I BETTER LOOK UNDER L.
HOW WONDERFUL! I LOVE YOU TOO!
OH NO! WHAT NOW?
IT'S A WHATCHAMACALLIT!

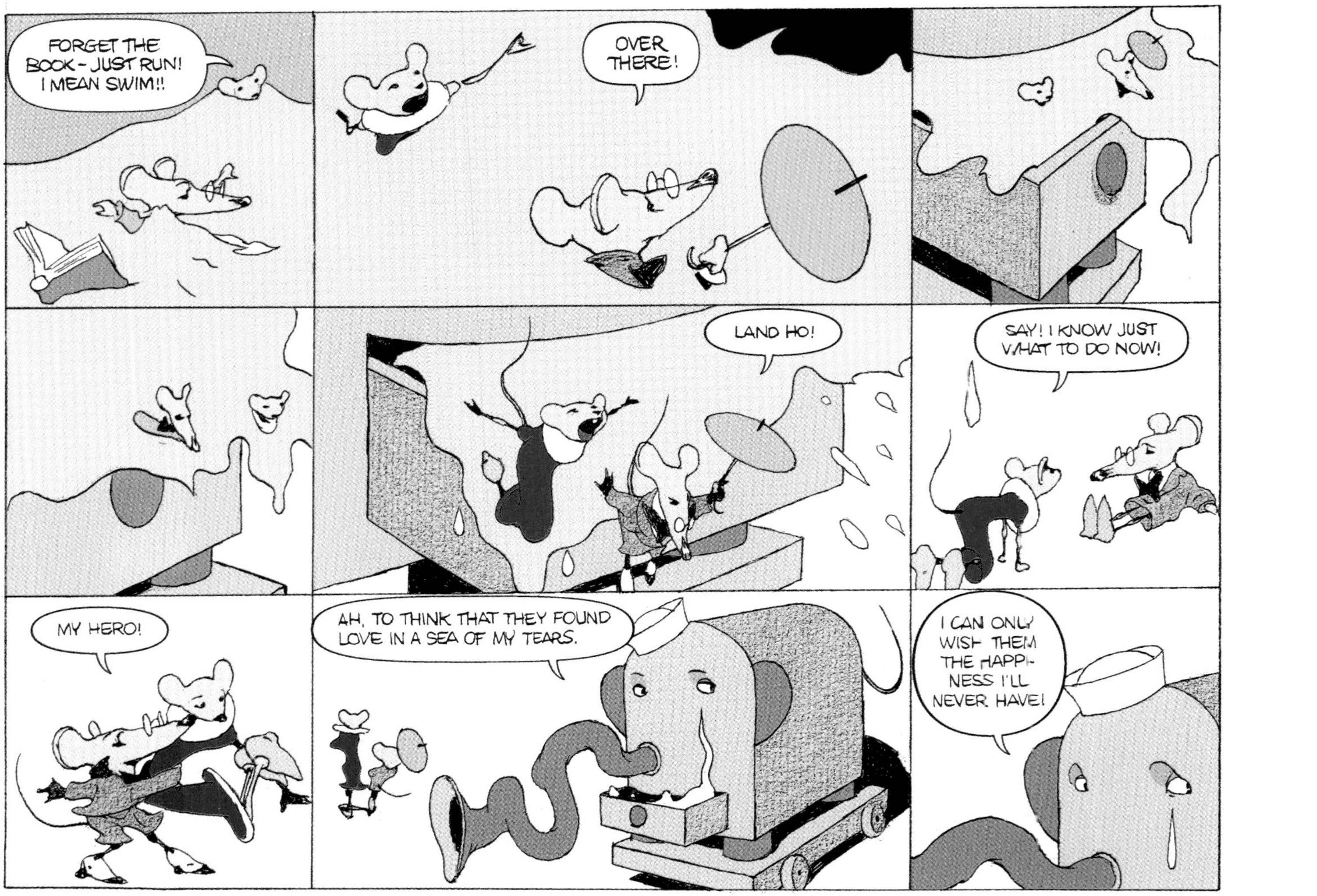
FORGET THE BOOK - JUST RUN! I MEAN SWIM!!
OVER THERE!
LAND HO!
SAY! I KNOW JUST WHAT TO DO NOW!
MY HERO!
AH, TO THINK THAT THEY FOUND LOVE IN A SEA OF MY TEARS.
I CAN ONLY WISH THEM THE HAPPI-NESS I'LL NEVER HAVE!

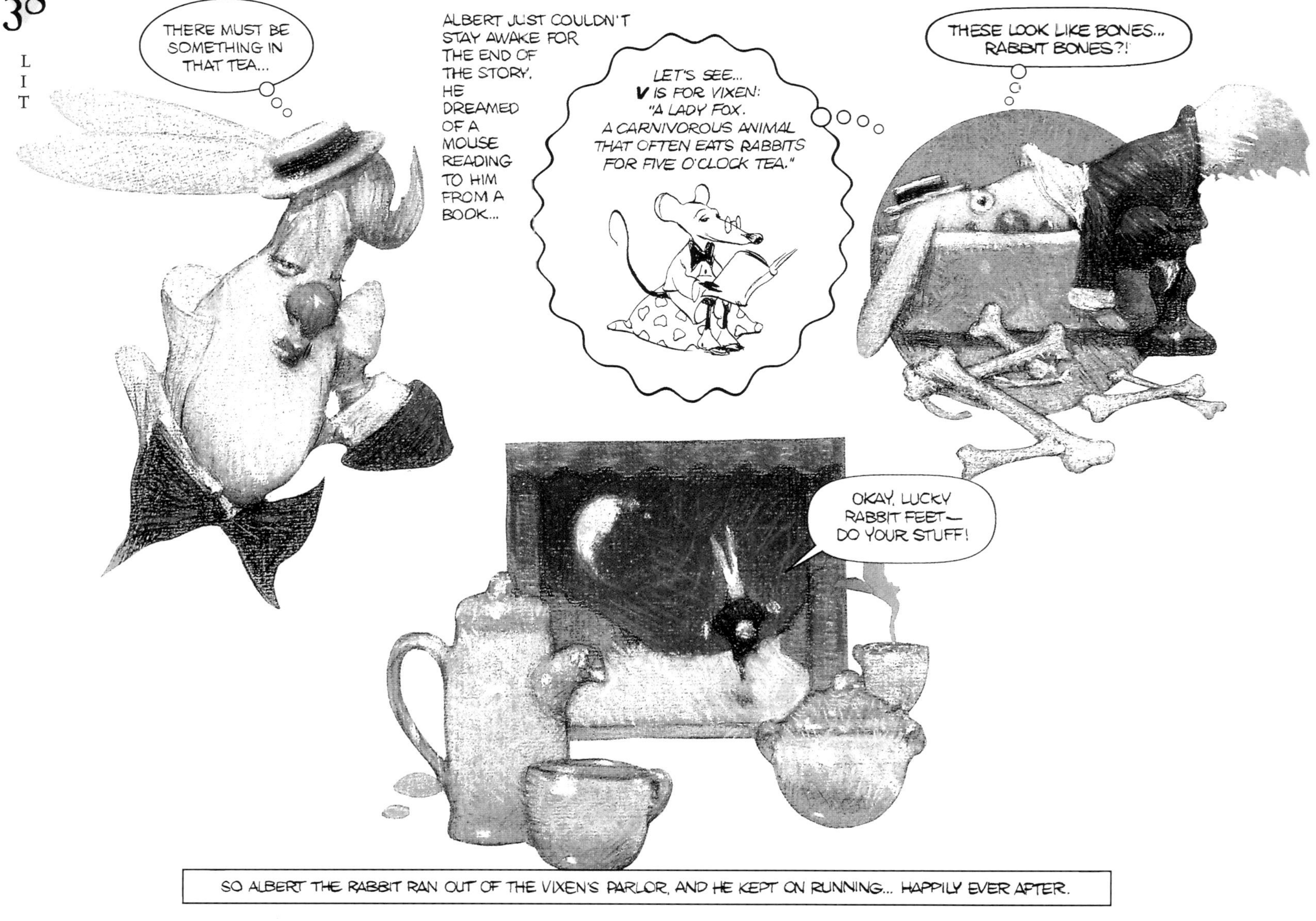
THERE MUST BE SOMETHING IN THAT TEA...
ALBERT JUST COULDN'T STAY AWAKE FOR THE END OF THE STORY. HE DREAMED OF A MOUSE READING TO HIM FROM A BOOK...
LET'S SEE... **V** IS FOR VIXEN: "A LADY FOX. A CARNIVOROUS ANIMAL THAT OFTEN EATS RABBITS FOR FIVE O'CLOCK TEA."
THESE LOOK LIKE BONES... RABBIT BONES?!
OKAY, LUCKY RABBIT FEET— DO YOUR STUFF!
SO ALBERT THE RABBIT RAN OUT OF THE VIXEN'S PARLOR, AND HE KEPT ON RUNNING... HAPPILY EVER AFTER.

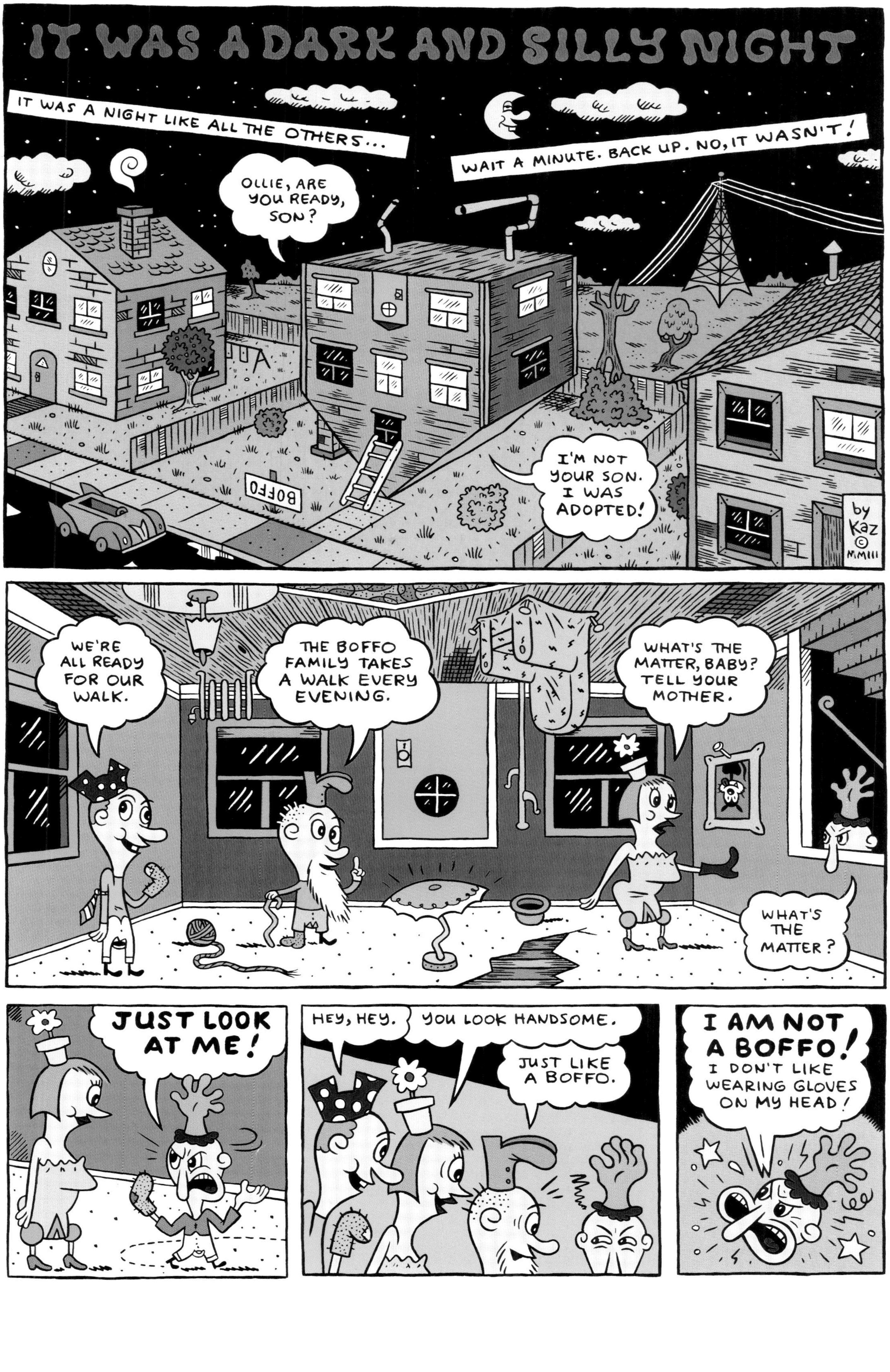
IT WAS A DARK AND SILLY NIGHT
IT WAS A NIGHT LIKE ALL THE OTHERS...
WAIT A MINUTE. BACK UP. NO, IT WASN'T!
OLLIE, ARE YOU READY, SON?
BOFFO
I'M NOT YOUR SON. I WAS ADOPTED!
by Kaz © MMIII
WE'RE ALL READY FOR OUR WALK.
THE BOFFO FAMILY TAKES A WALK EVERY EVENING.
WHAT'S THE MATTER, BABY? TELL YOUR MOTHER.
WHAT'S THE MATTER?
JUST LOOK AT ME!
HEY, HEY.
YOU LOOK HANDSOME.
JUST LIKE A BOFFO.
I AM NOT A BOFFO!
I DON'T LIKE WEARING GLOVES ON MY HEAD!

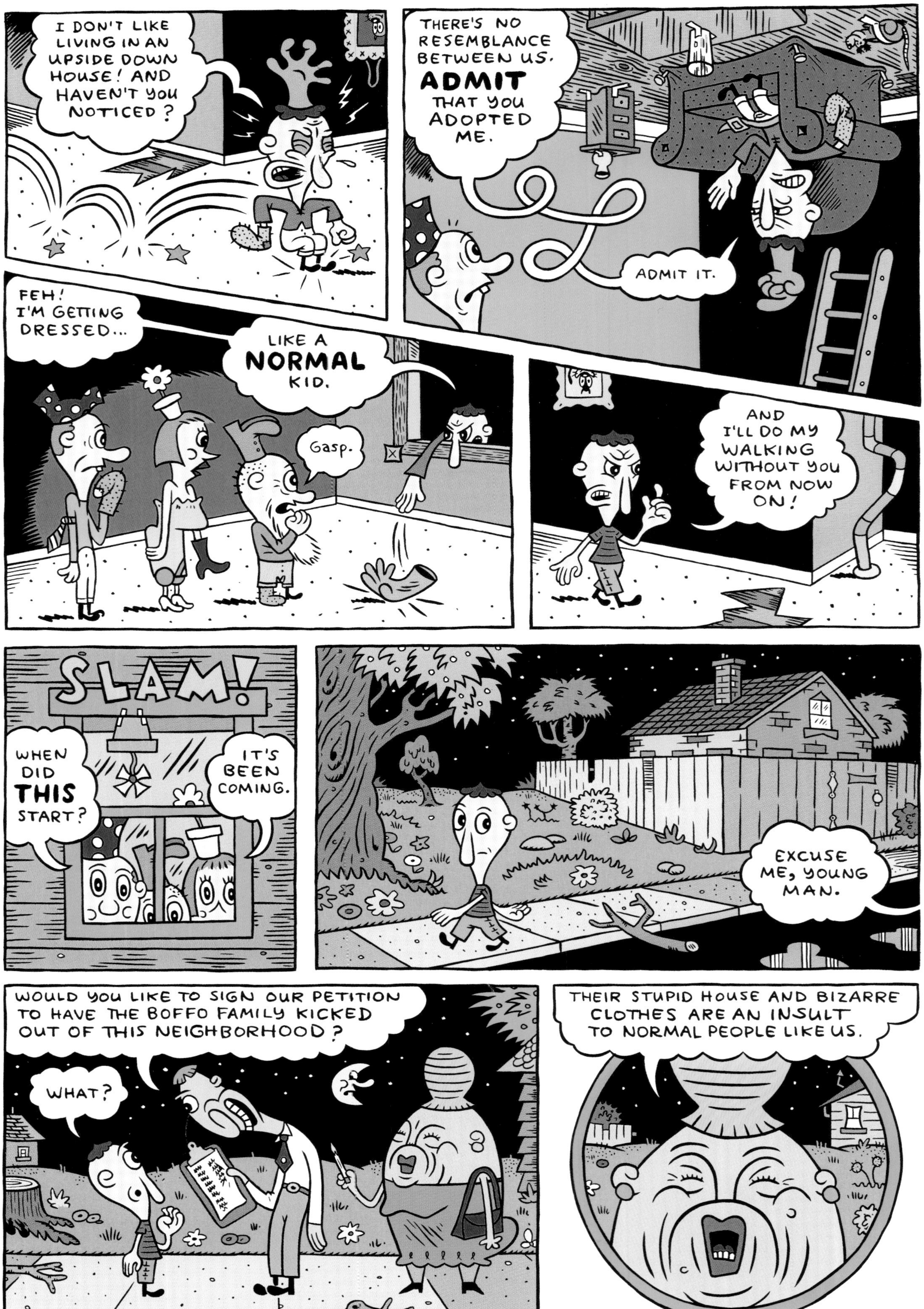
I DON'T LIKE LIVING IN AN UPSIDE DOWN HOUSE! AND HAVEN'T YOU NOTICED?
THERE'S NO RESEMBLANCE BETWEEN US. ADMIT THAT YOU ADOPTED ME.
ADMIT IT.
FEH! I'M GETTING DRESSED...
LIKE A NORMAL KID.
Gasp.
AND I'LL DO MY WALKING WITHOUT YOU FROM NOW ON!
SLAM!
WHEN DID THIS START?
IT'S BEEN COMING.
EXCUSE ME, YOUNG MAN.
WOULD YOU LIKE TO SIGN OUR PETITION TO HAVE THE BOFFO FAMILY KICKED OUT OF THIS NEIGHBORHOOD?
WHAT?
THEIR STUPID HOUSE AND BIZARRE CLOTHES ARE AN INSULT TO NORMAL PEOPLE LIKE US.

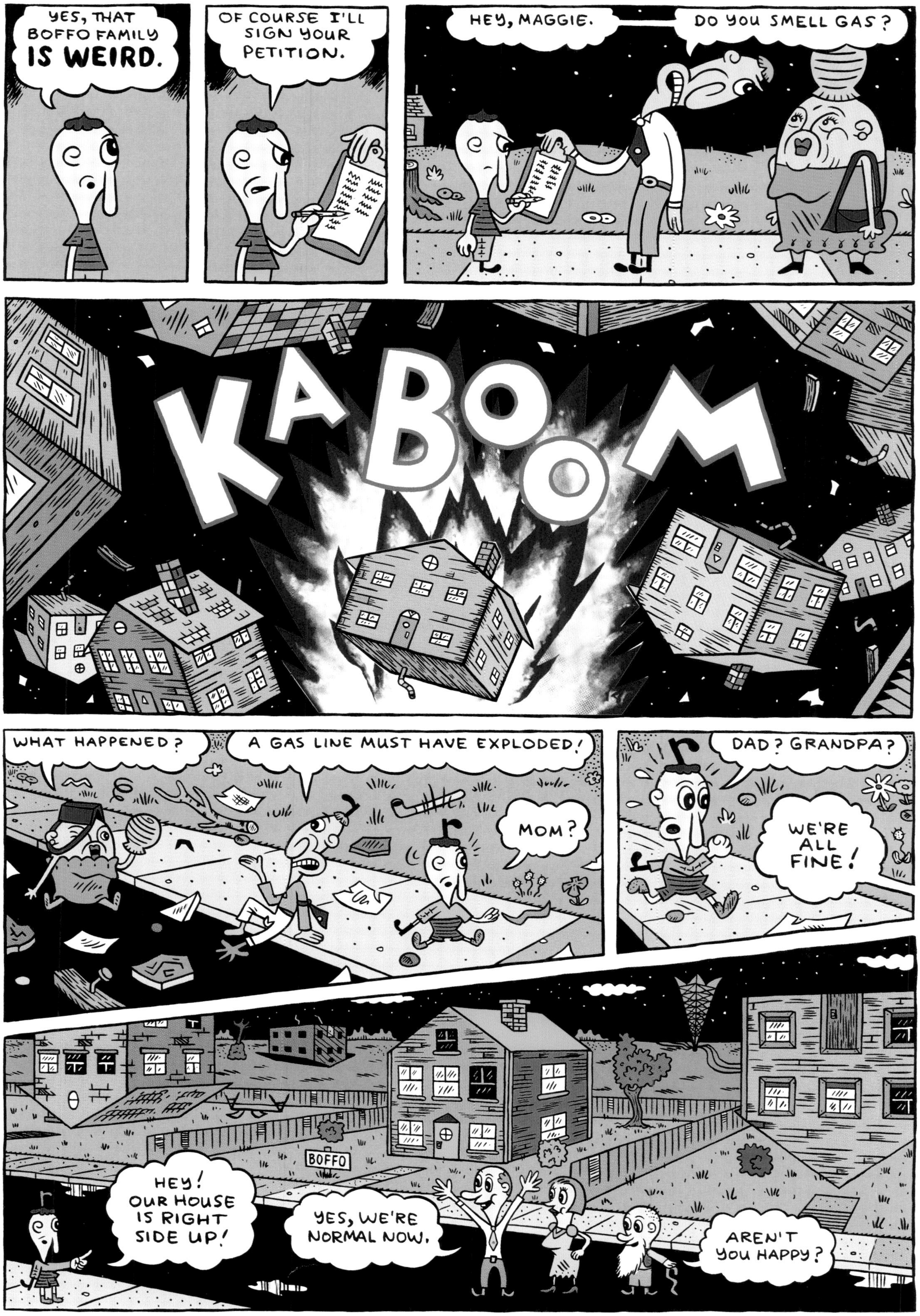
YES, THAT BOFFO FAMILY IS WEIRD.
OF COURSE I'LL SIGN YOUR PETITION.
HEY, MAGGIE.
DO YOU SMELL GAS?
KABOOM
WHAT HAPPENED?
A GAS LINE MUST HAVE EXPLODED!
MOM?
DAD? GRANDPA?
WE'RE ALL FINE!
BOFFO
HEY! OUR HOUSE IS RIGHT SIDE UP!
YES, WE'RE NORMAL NOW.
AREN'T YOU HAPPY?

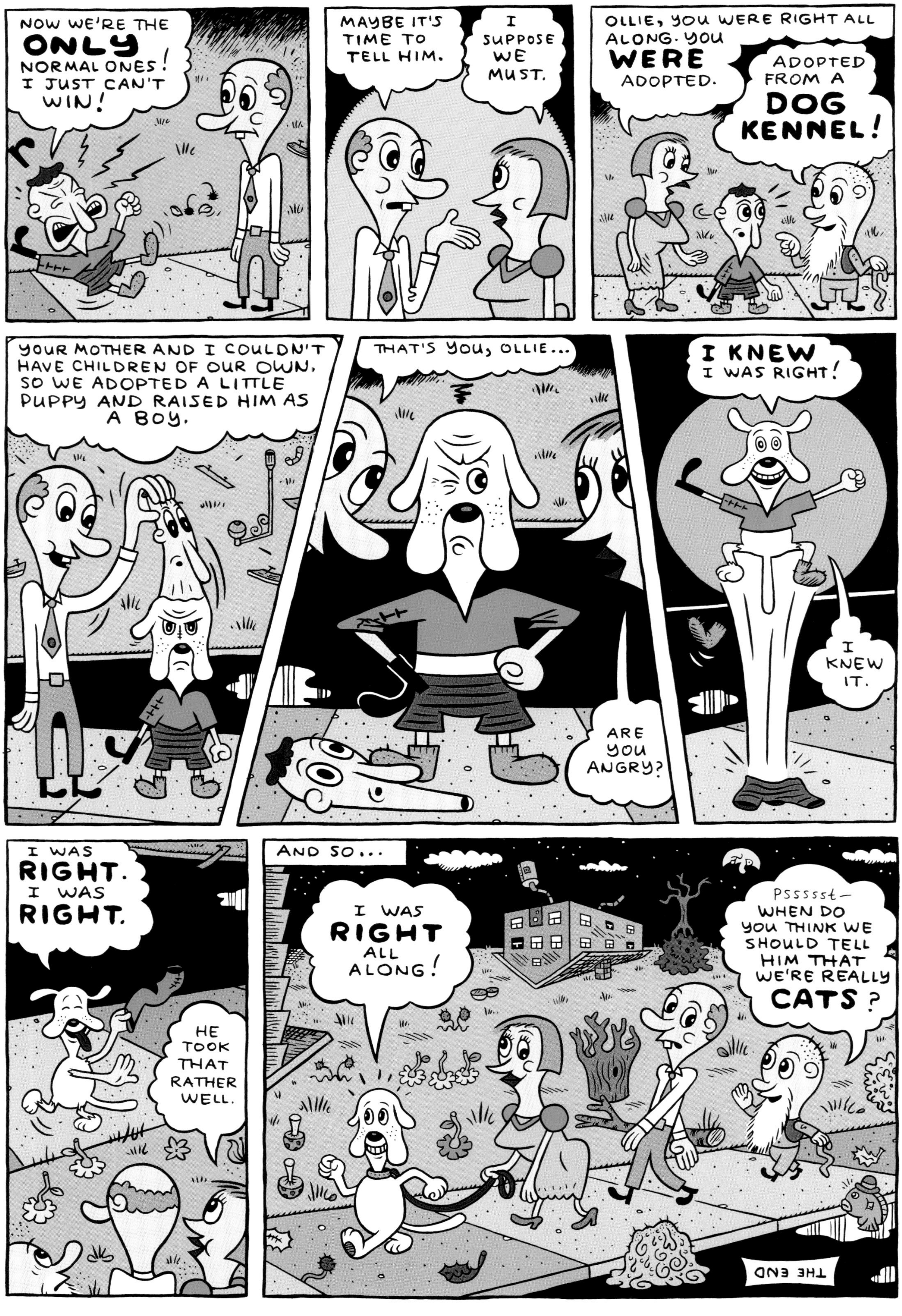

NOW WE'RE THE ONLY NORMAL ONES! I JUST CAN'T WIN!
MAYBE IT'S TIME TO TELL HIM.
I SUPPOSE WE MUST.
OLLIE, YOU WERE RIGHT ALL ALONG. YOU WERE ADOPTED.
ADOPTED FROM A DOG KENNEL!
YOUR MOTHER AND I COULDN'T HAVE CHILDREN OF OUR OWN, SO WE ADOPTED A LITTLE PUPPY AND RAISED HIM AS A BOY.
THAT'S YOU, OLLIE...
ARE YOU ANGRY?
I KNEW I WAS RIGHT!
I KNEW IT.
I WAS RIGHT. I WAS RIGHT.
HE TOOK THAT RATHER WELL.
AND SO...
I WAS RIGHT ALL ALONG!
Pssssst— WHEN DO YOU THINK WE SHOULD TELL HIM THAT WE'RE REALLY CATS?
THE END

barbara mcclintock

IT WAS A DARK AND SILLY NIGHT...

as the bears frolicked under the moon. Find the 12 differences between the two pictures. Warning: the last 4 are for the super sleuths among you.

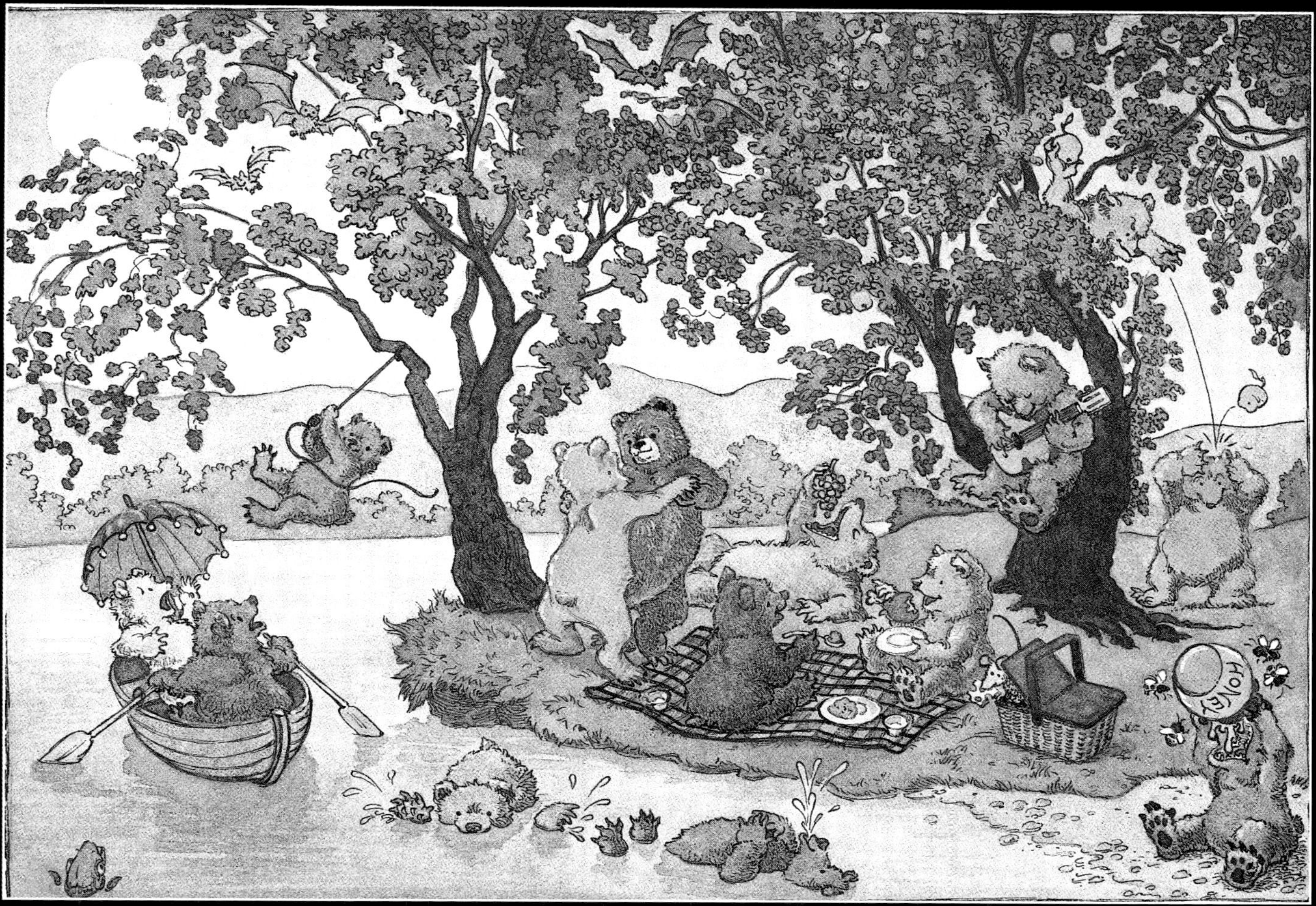
HONEY

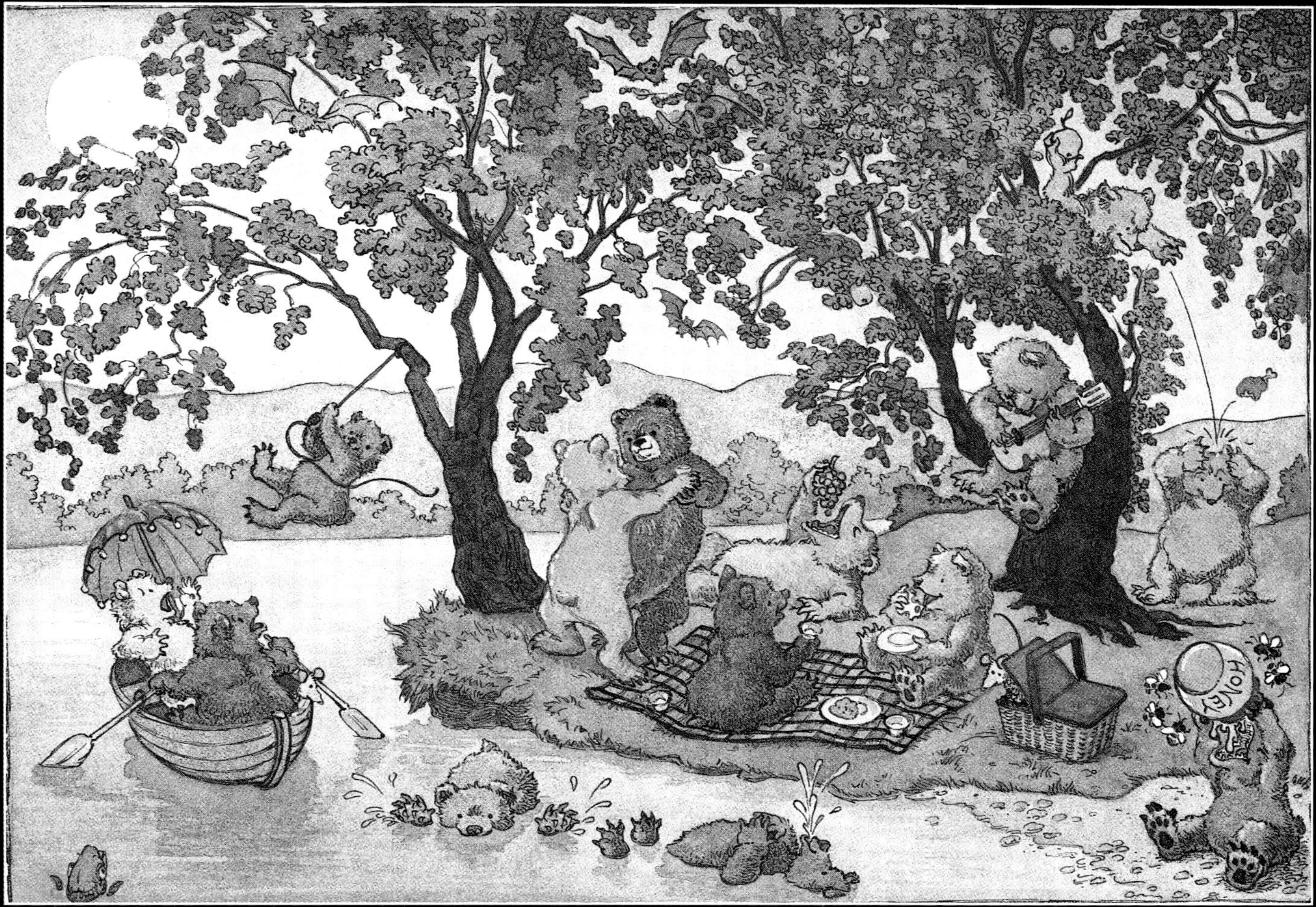
HONEY

(You can check your answers at the end of the book.)

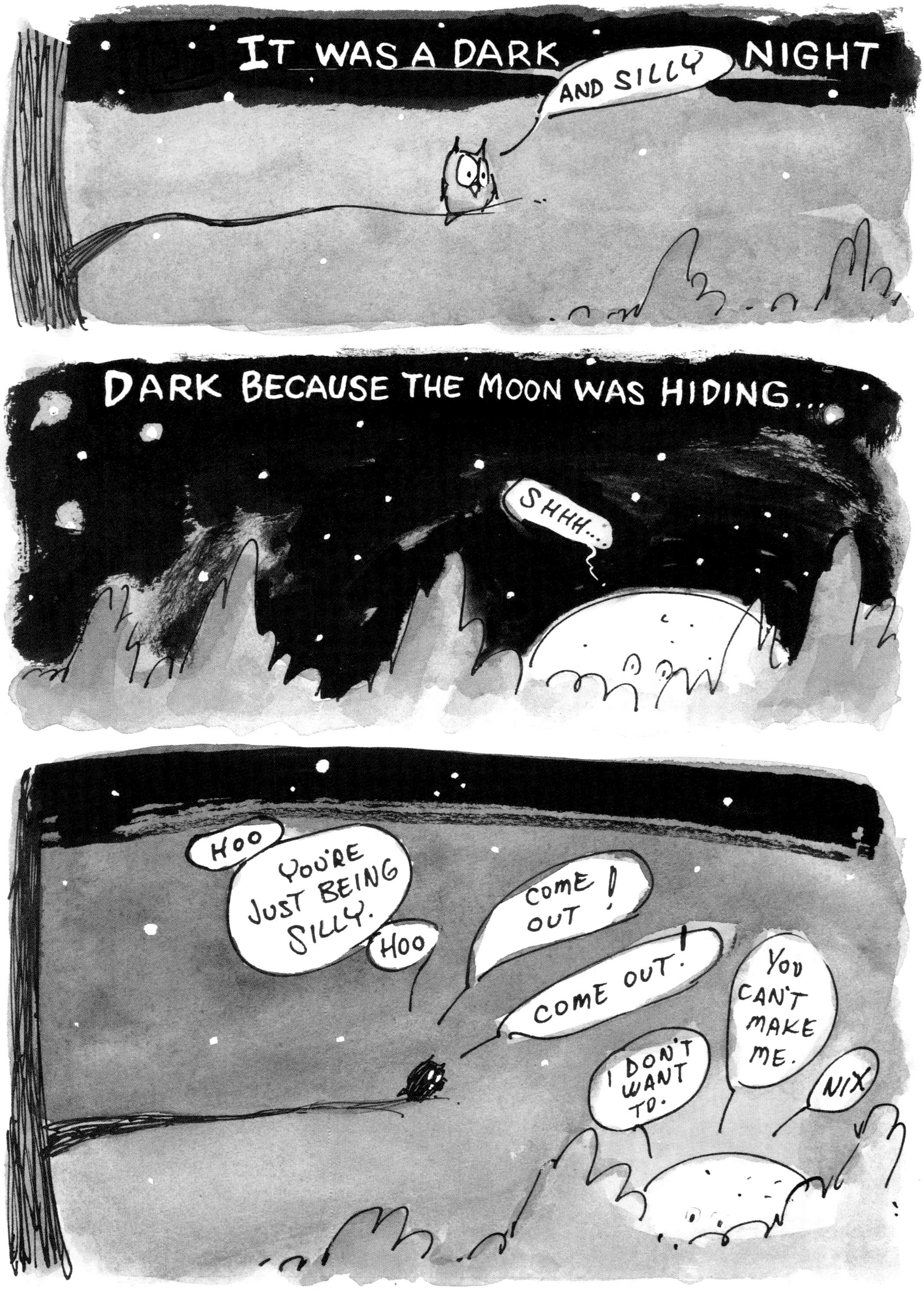
IT WAS A DARK
AND SILLY
NIGHT
DARK BECAUSE THE MOON WAS HIDING...
SHHH...
HOO
YOU'RE JUST BEING SILLY.
HOO
COME OUT!
COME OUT!
I DON'T WANT TO.
YOU CAN'T MAKE ME.
NIX
NO MOON

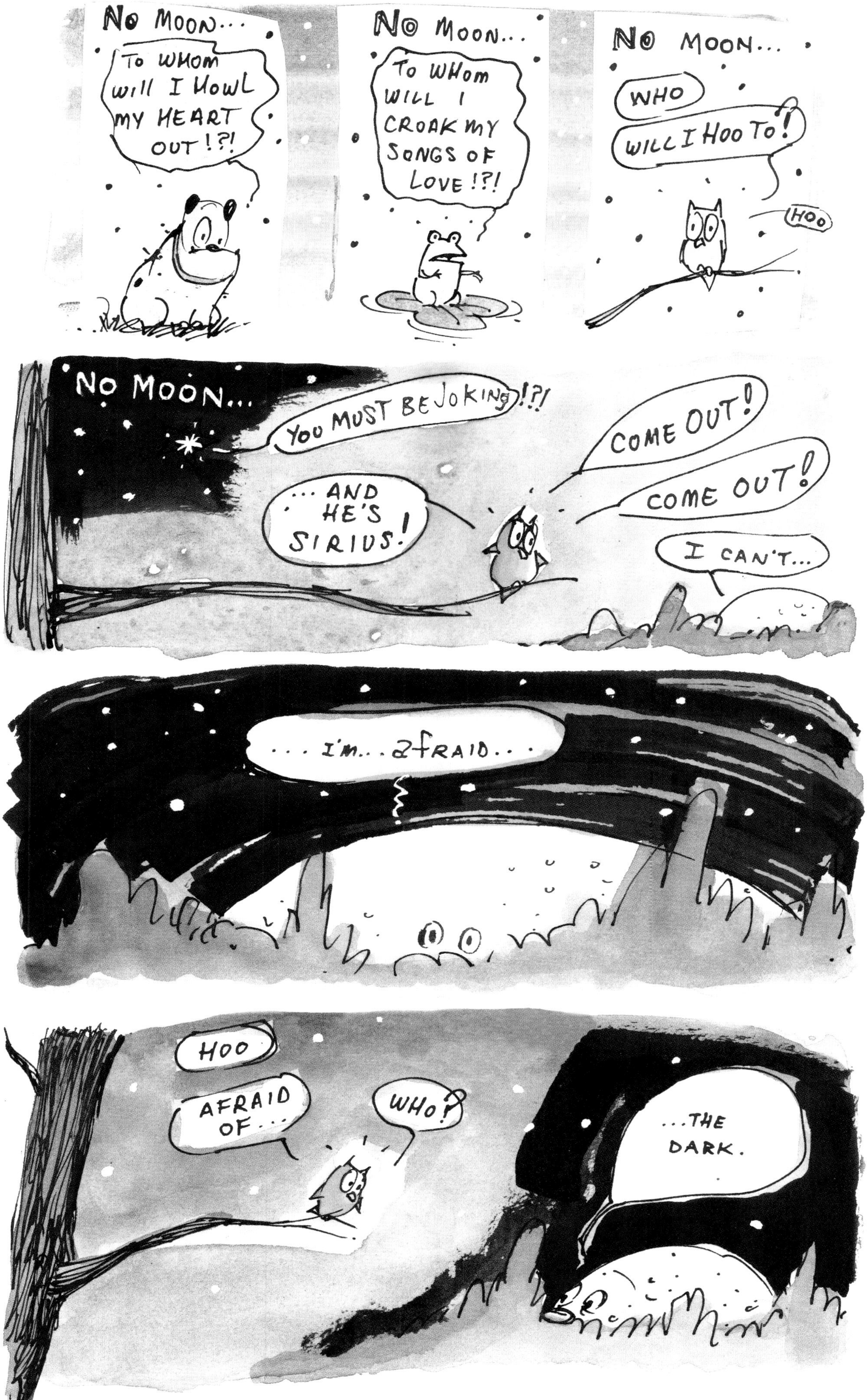
NO MOON...
TO WHOM WILL I HOWL MY HEART OUT!?!
NO MOON...
TO WHOM WILL I CROAK MY SONGS OF LOVE!?!
NO MOON...
WHO
WILL I HOO TO!
HOO
NO MOON...
YOU MUST BE JOKING!?!
...AND HE'S SIRIUS!
COME OUT!
COME OUT!
I CAN'T...
...I'M...AFRAID...
HOO
AFRAID OF...
WHO?
...THE DARK.

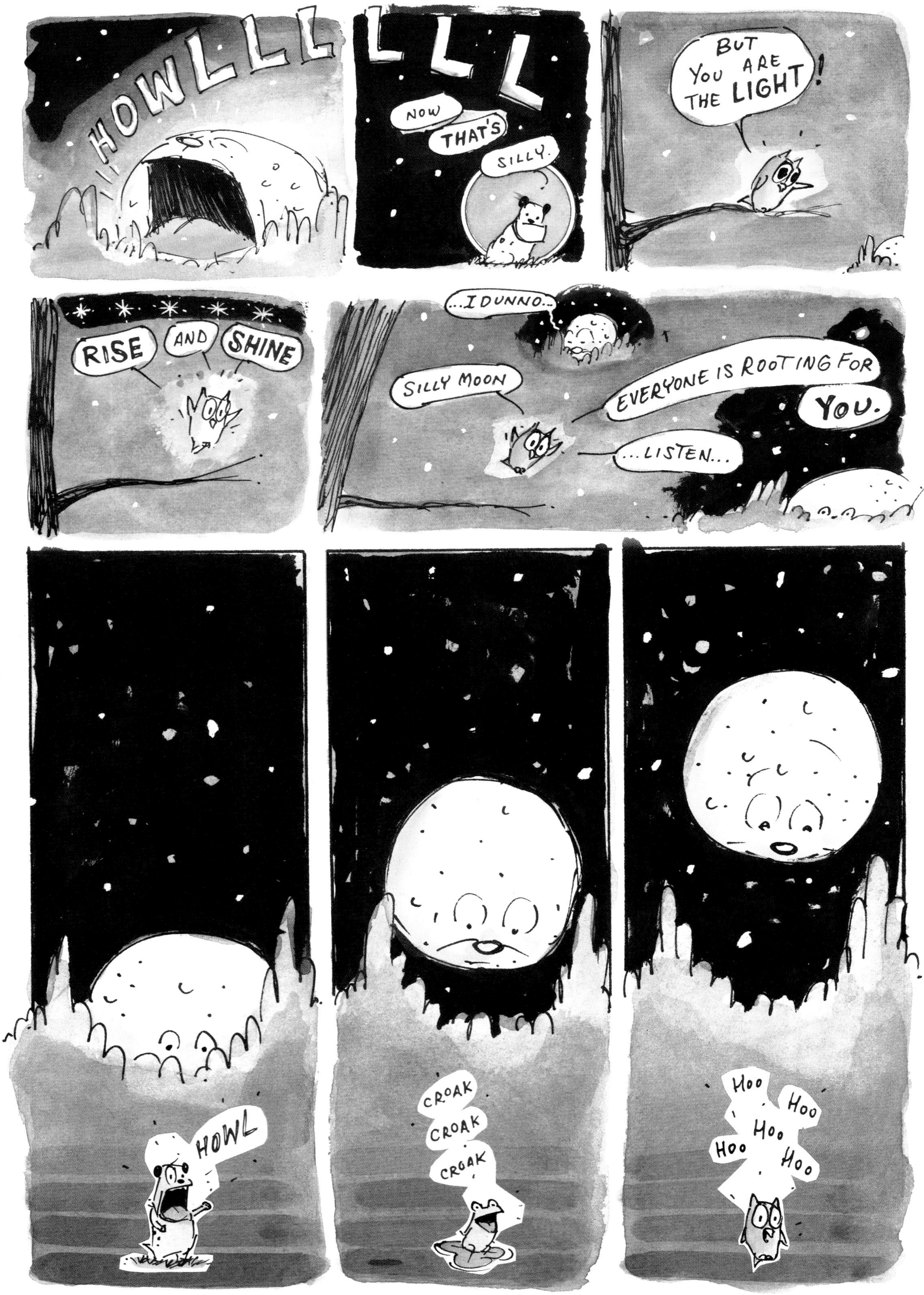
HOWLLL
LLL
NOW
THAT'S
SILLY.
BUT YOU ARE THE LIGHT!
RISE
AND
SHINE
...I DUNNO...
SILLY MOON
EVERYONE IS ROOTING FOR YOU.
...LISTEN...
HOWL
CROAK
CROAK
CROAK
HOO
HOO
HOO
HOO
HOO

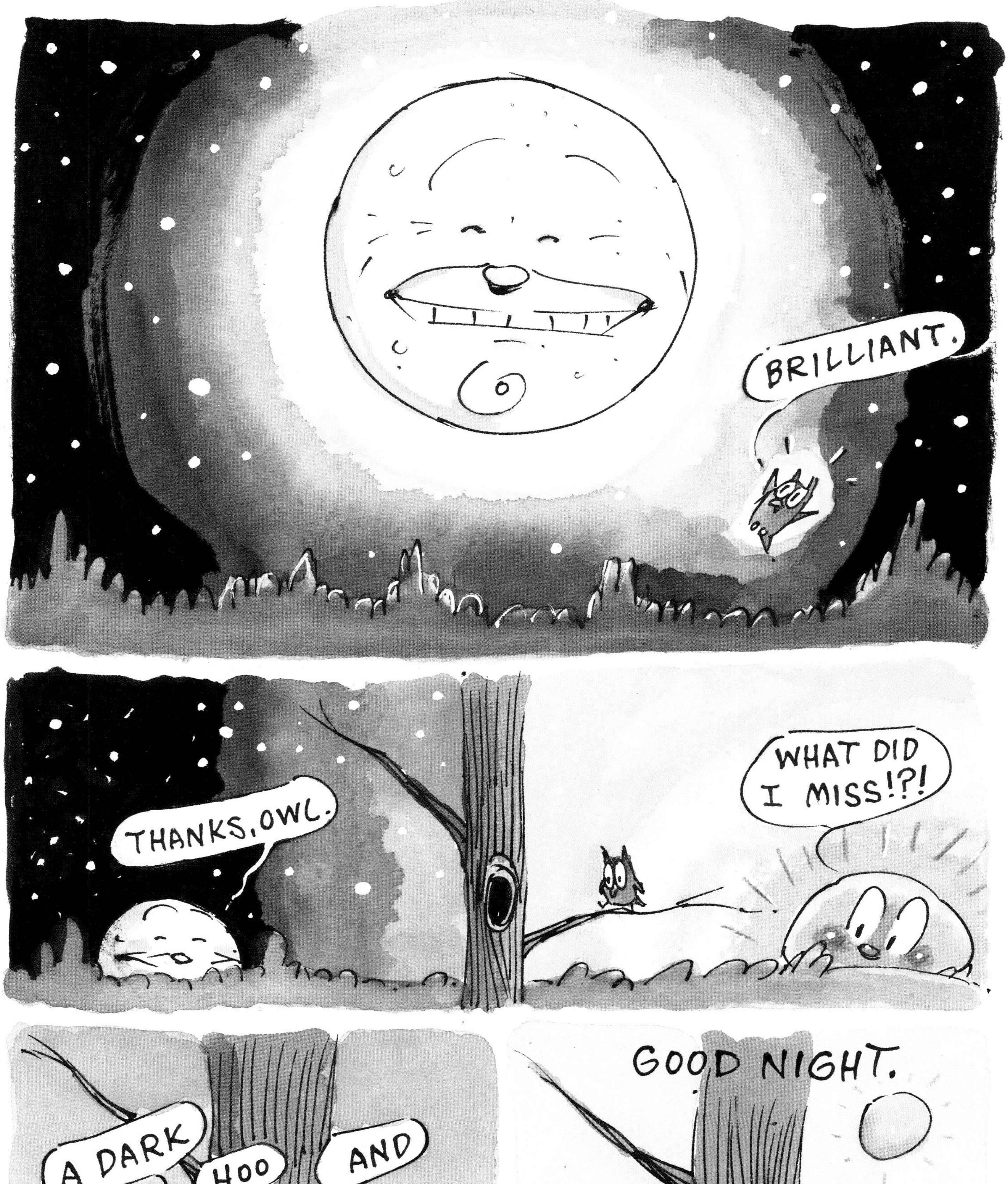
BRILLIANT.
THANKS, OWL.
WHAT DID I MISS!?!
A DARK
HOO
AND
SILLY
HOO
GOOD NIGHT.
Z

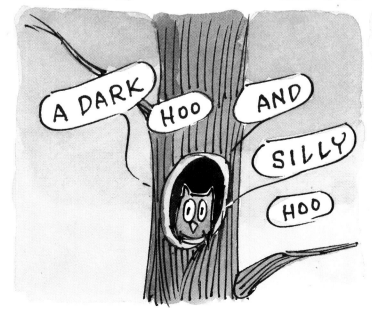

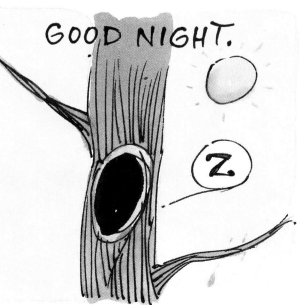

r. sikoryak and ___

Make your own dark and silly tale!

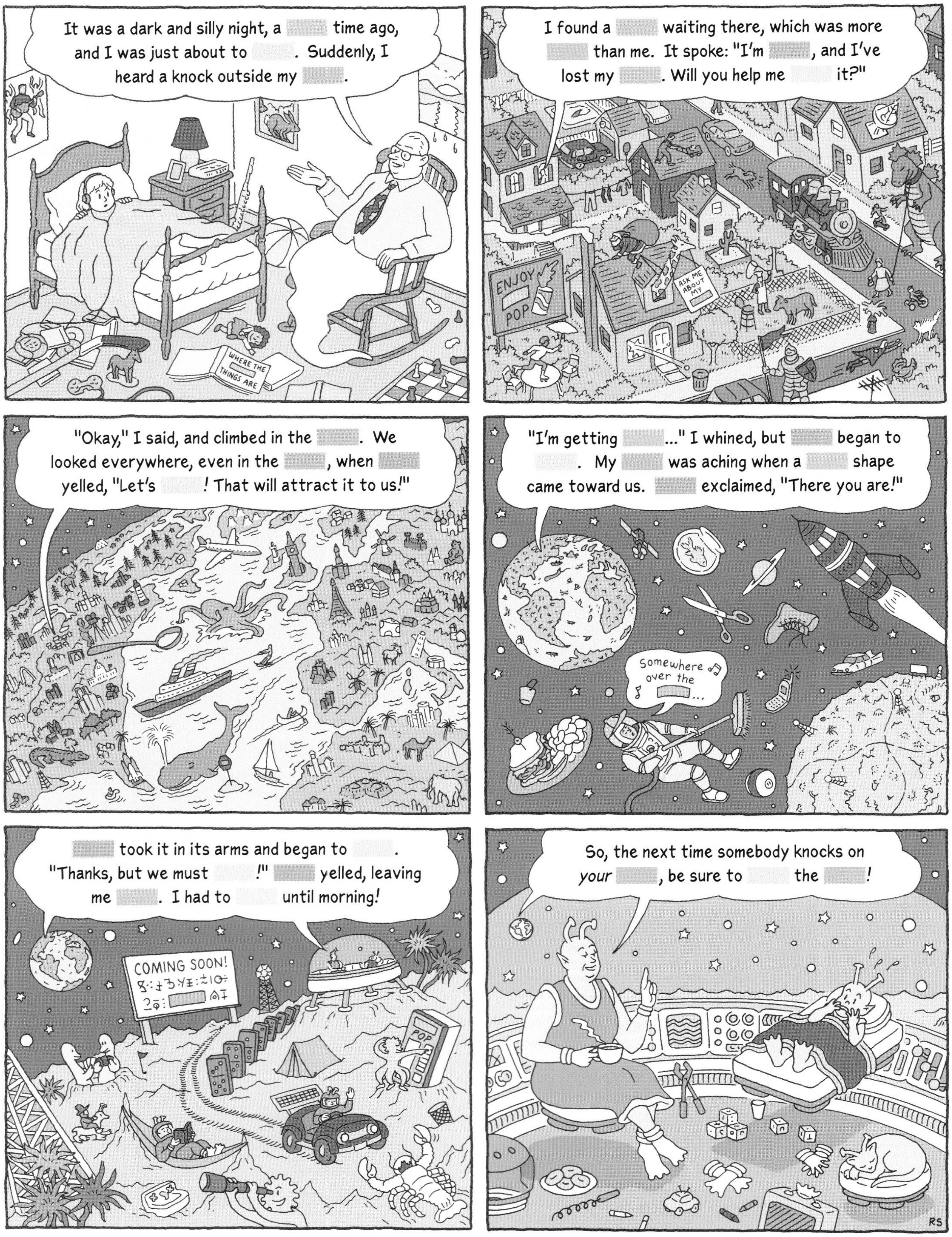
It was a dark and silly night, a ___ time ago, and I was just about to ___. Suddenly, I heard a knock outside my ___.
WHERE THE ___ THINGS ARE
I found a ___ waiting there, which was more ___ than me. It spoke: "I'm ___, and I've lost my ___. Will you help me ___ it?"
ENJOY ___ POP
ASK ME ABOUT MY ___
"Okay," I said, and climbed in the ___. We looked everywhere, even in the ___, when ___ yelled, "Let's ___! That will attract it to us!"
"I'm getting ___..." I whined, but ___ began to ___. My ___ was aching when a ___ shape came toward us. ___ exclaimed, "There you are!"
Somewhere over the ___...
___ took it in its arms and began to ___. "Thanks, but we must ___!" ___ yelled, leaving me ___. I had to ___ until morning!
COMING SOON!
POP
So, the next time somebody knocks on *your* ___, be sure to ___ the ___!
RS

First you'll need to make a list of words. *(Be sure to write on a separate piece of paper so you can play again and again!)* Choose 8 BLUE WORDS (nouns): these can be any person, place, or thing, such as "father," "bedroom," or "toy"; 8 YELLOW WORDS (verbs): action words, such as "talk," "eat," or "play"; 5 GREEN WORDS (adjectives): words that describe something, such as "happy," "small," or "bright." Finally, you'll need 1 PURPLE WORD (name): such as "Britney," "Spot," or your own. Once you've made your list, read the finished story by substituting your words in the colored blanks.

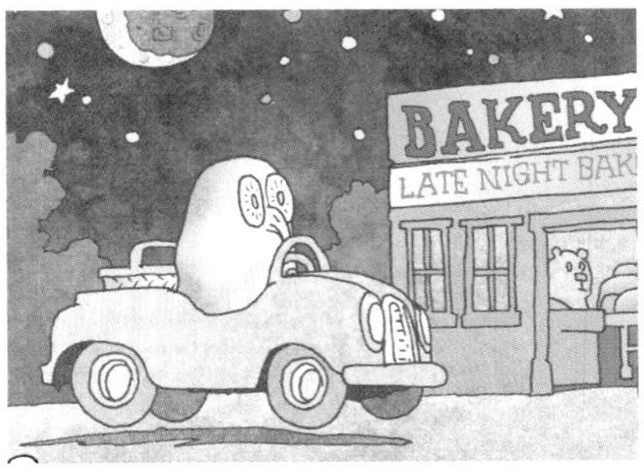
BAKERY

ANSWERS

PAGE 22

E, F, C, A, D, B

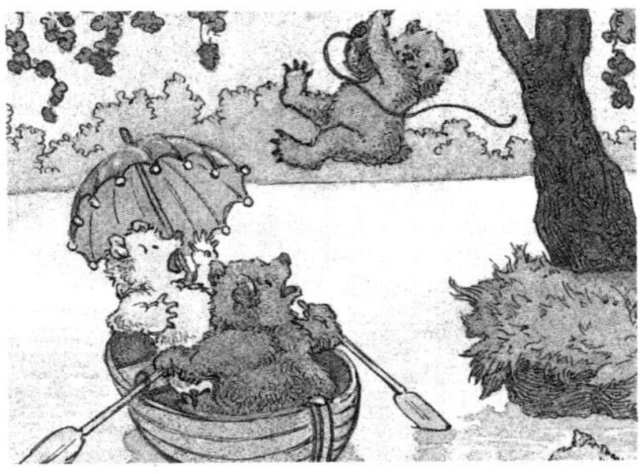

PAGE 43

1. The thrown apple became a chicken leg. 2. Another bee wants honey. 3. The mouse in the picnic basket lost her cheese. 4. A brown bear is eating her cheese. 5. A bear sitting on the blanket has a cup of water. 6. The dancing bears are sharing a drink. 7. The rowboat has a stowaway mouse. 8. A bat near the sun has disappeared.

SUPER SLEUTH ANSWERS: 9. The umbrella lost some tassels. 10. The swimming gray bear's left paw was changed. 11. A bat has appeared above the dancing bears. 12. One more apple has grown in the tree.

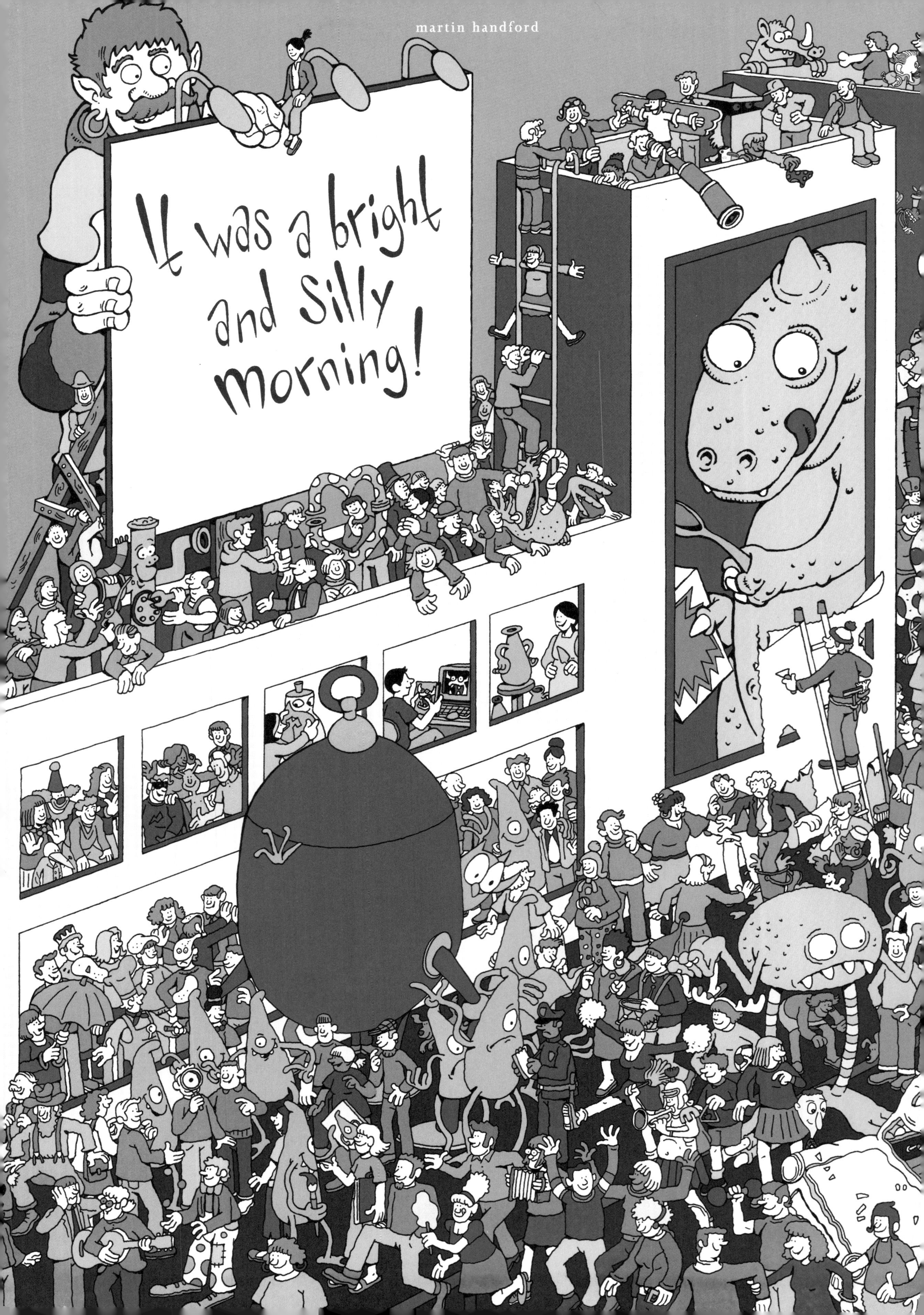
It was a bright
and silly
morning!